I0771357

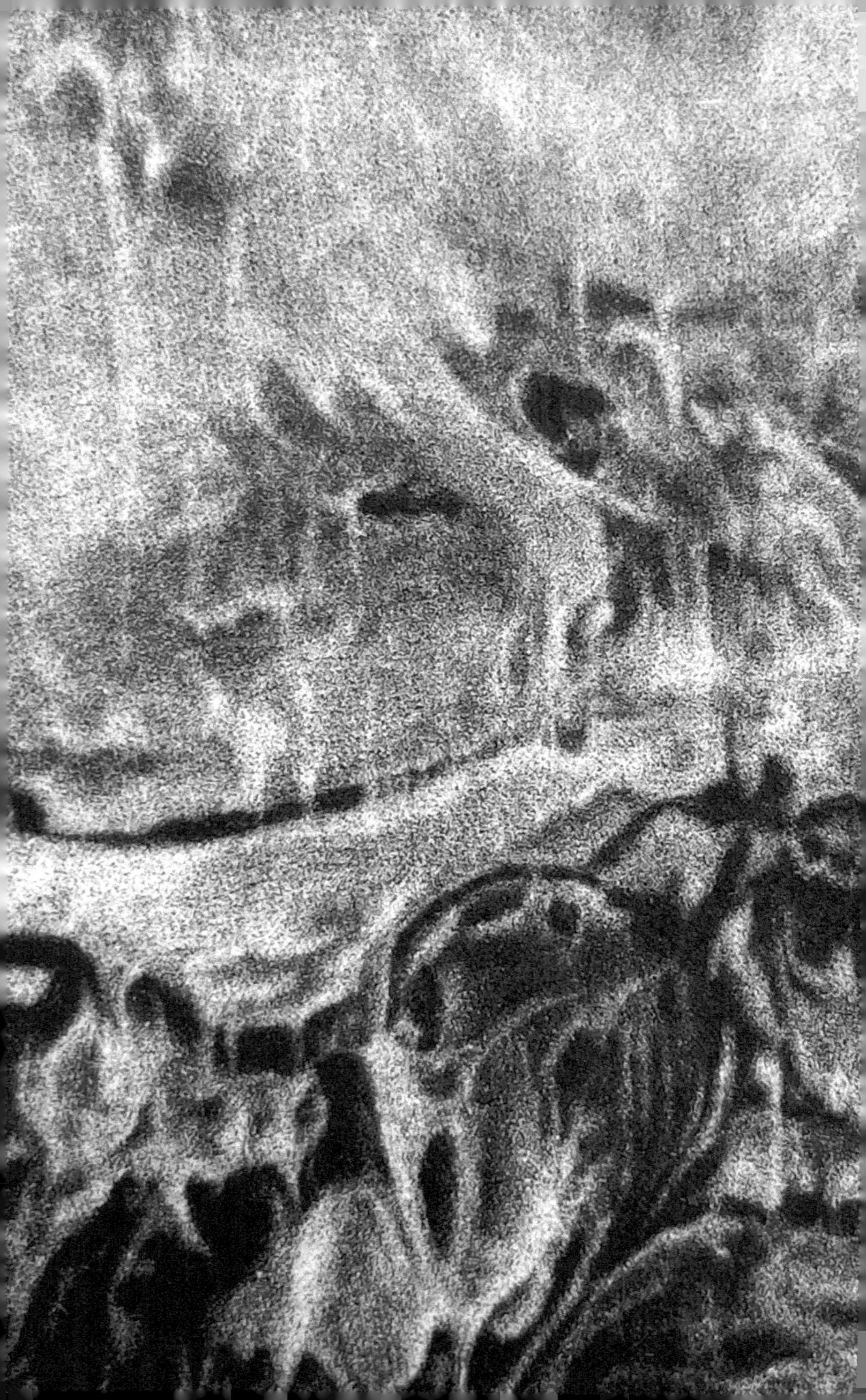

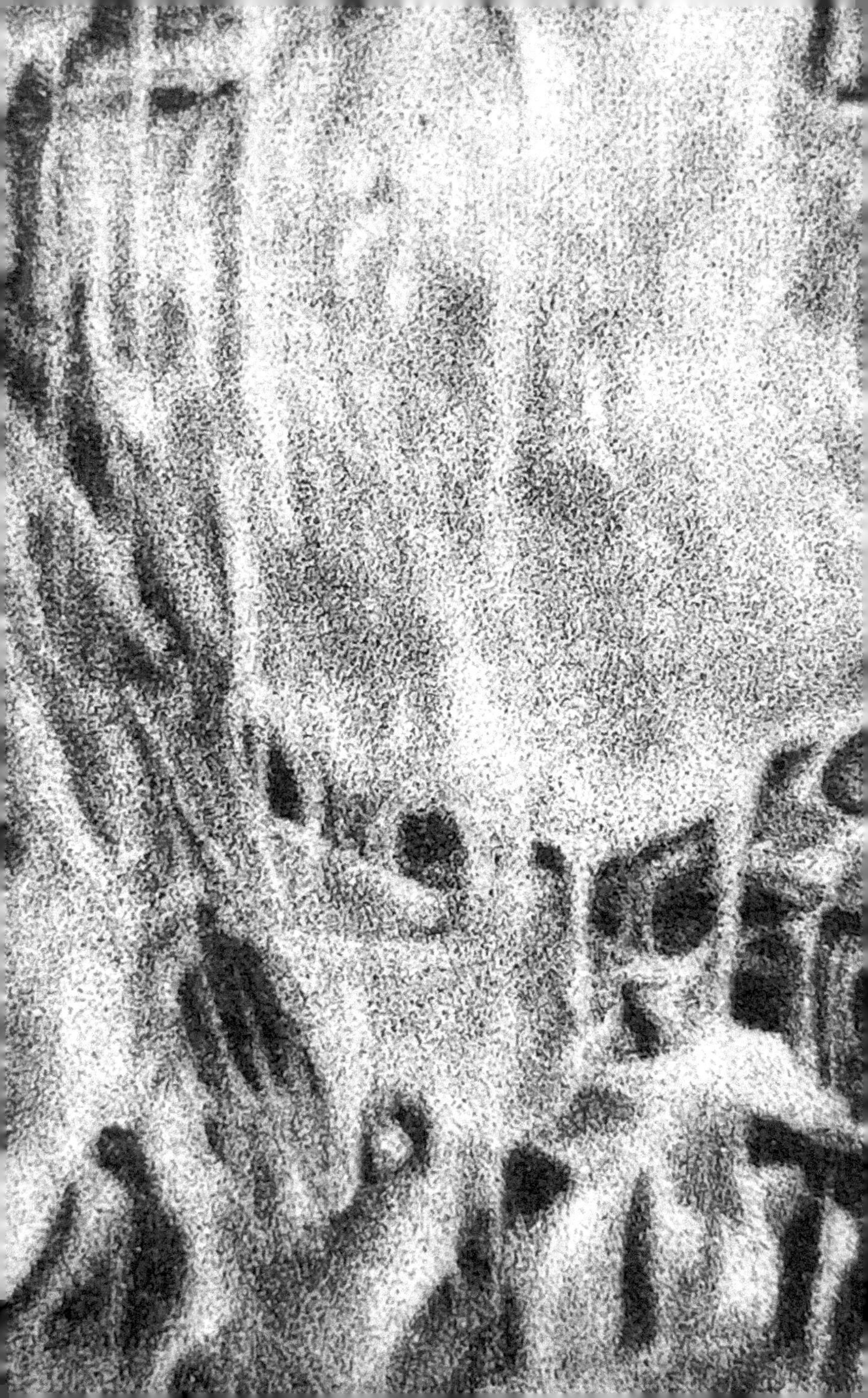

The Genocide House

Robert   Kloss

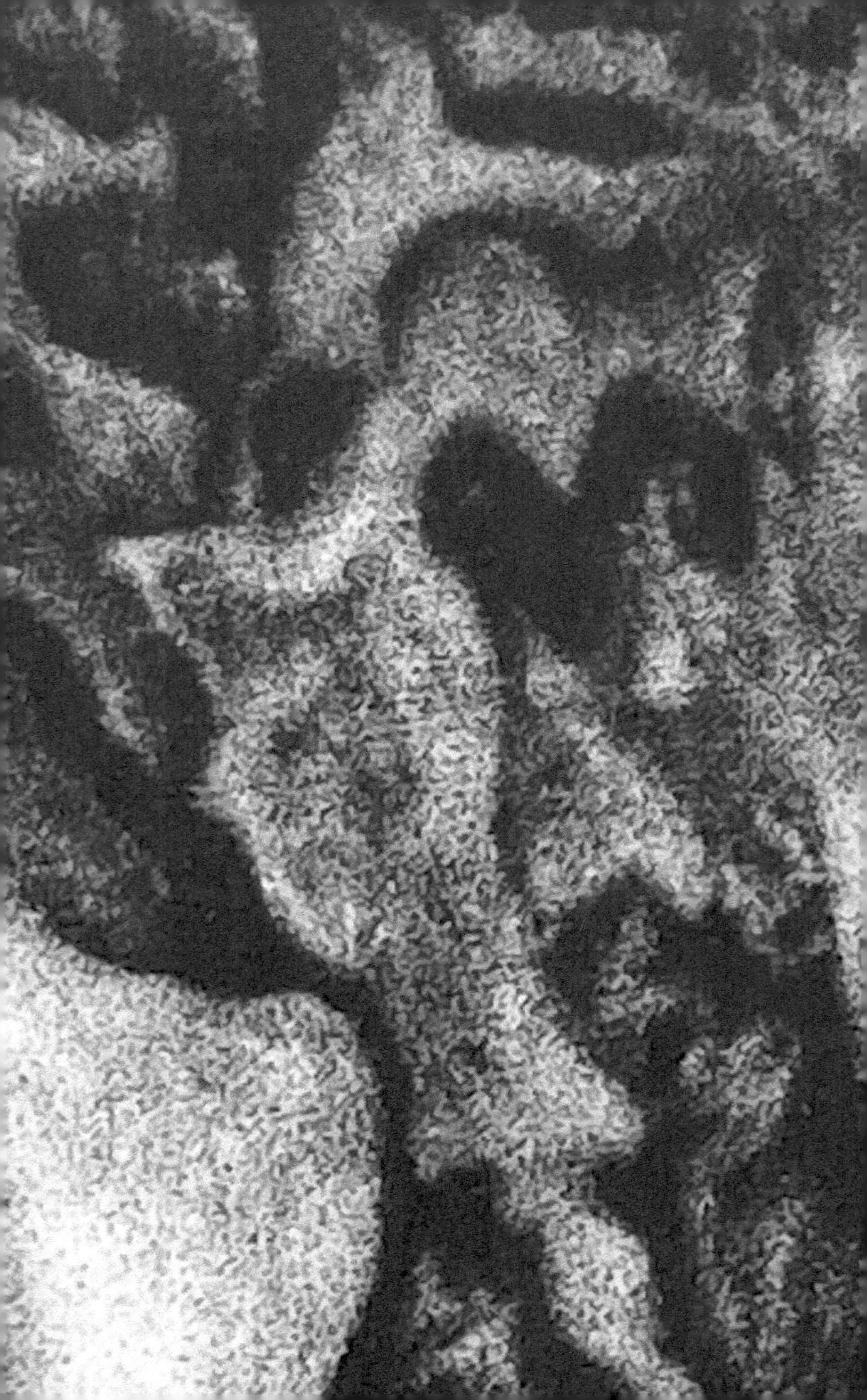

Published by Bridge Books, 2858 W. Belle Plaine Ave., #3, Chicago, IL, U.S.A
bridge-books.org

ISBN: 979-8-9879330-4-6
Library of Congress CIP #: 2024945501

Cover Image: *Record of Wear (detail)*, Devon Stackonis 2021. Mezzotint intaglio print on Zerkall paper.

Interior Chapter Images: Close up detail passages from nine successive mezzotint state impressions.

Cover and interior design by Michael Workman Studio.

This book was typeset using Adobe Caslon Pro, Filosophia OT, Park Lane and Source Sans Pro typefaces and is printed on acid-free paper by Ingram Spark.

Notes on production: In the mezzotint printmaking process, a copper plate is first prepared with a semicircular, toothed chisel to hold a field of ink. The image is developed by scraping and burnishing into the surface of the plate, so that areas may express a range of tones. In this sequence of nine state impressions, the plate is further scraped down between printing, resulting in a thinning and softening of the tonal image. This gradual wearing down of the material by handheld tools alongside the expected wear and degradation of a mezzotint plate printed many times over yields atmospheric, abstract passages. This piece addresses the physical lifespan of the medium itself as well as the impermanence of the human body.

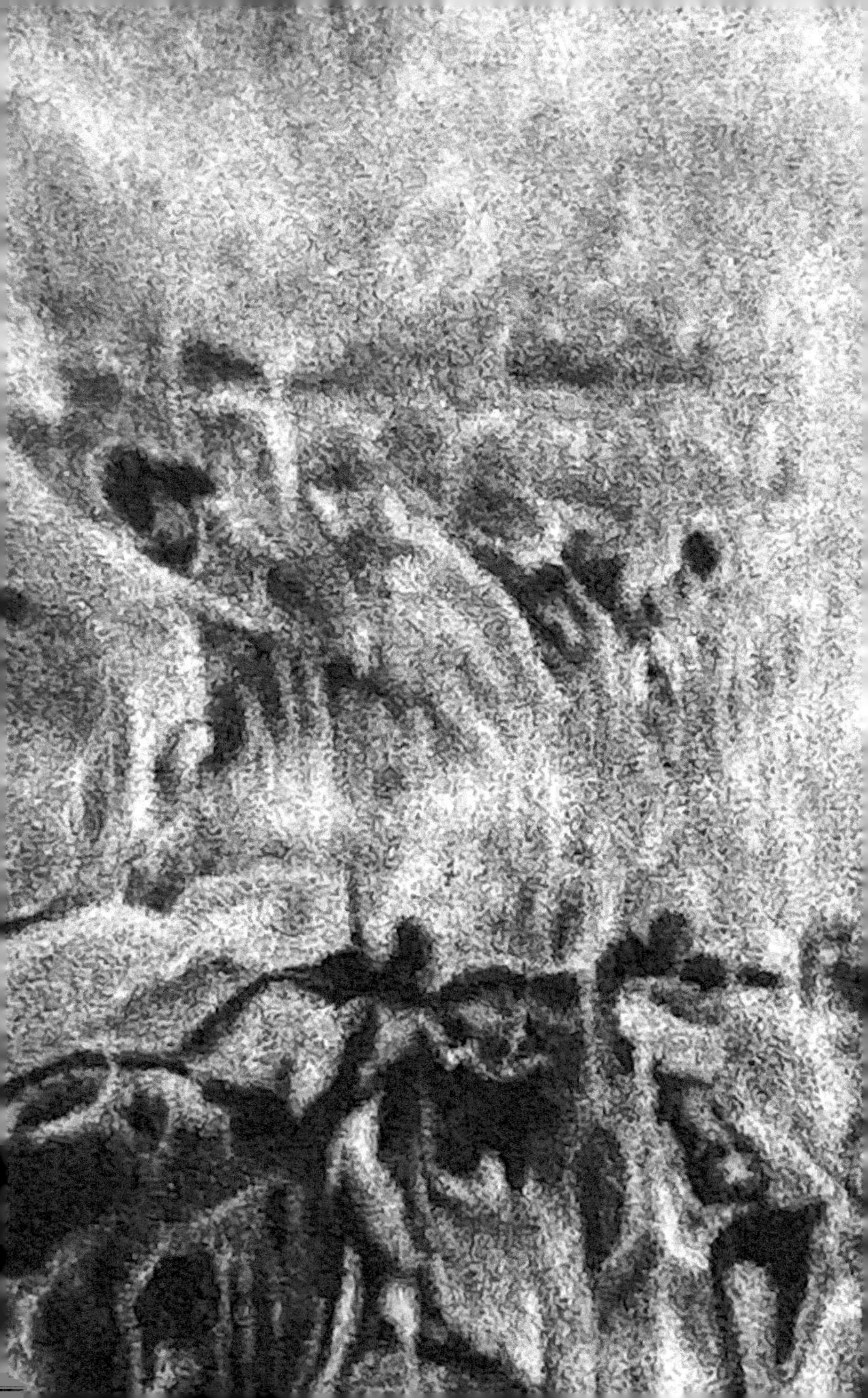

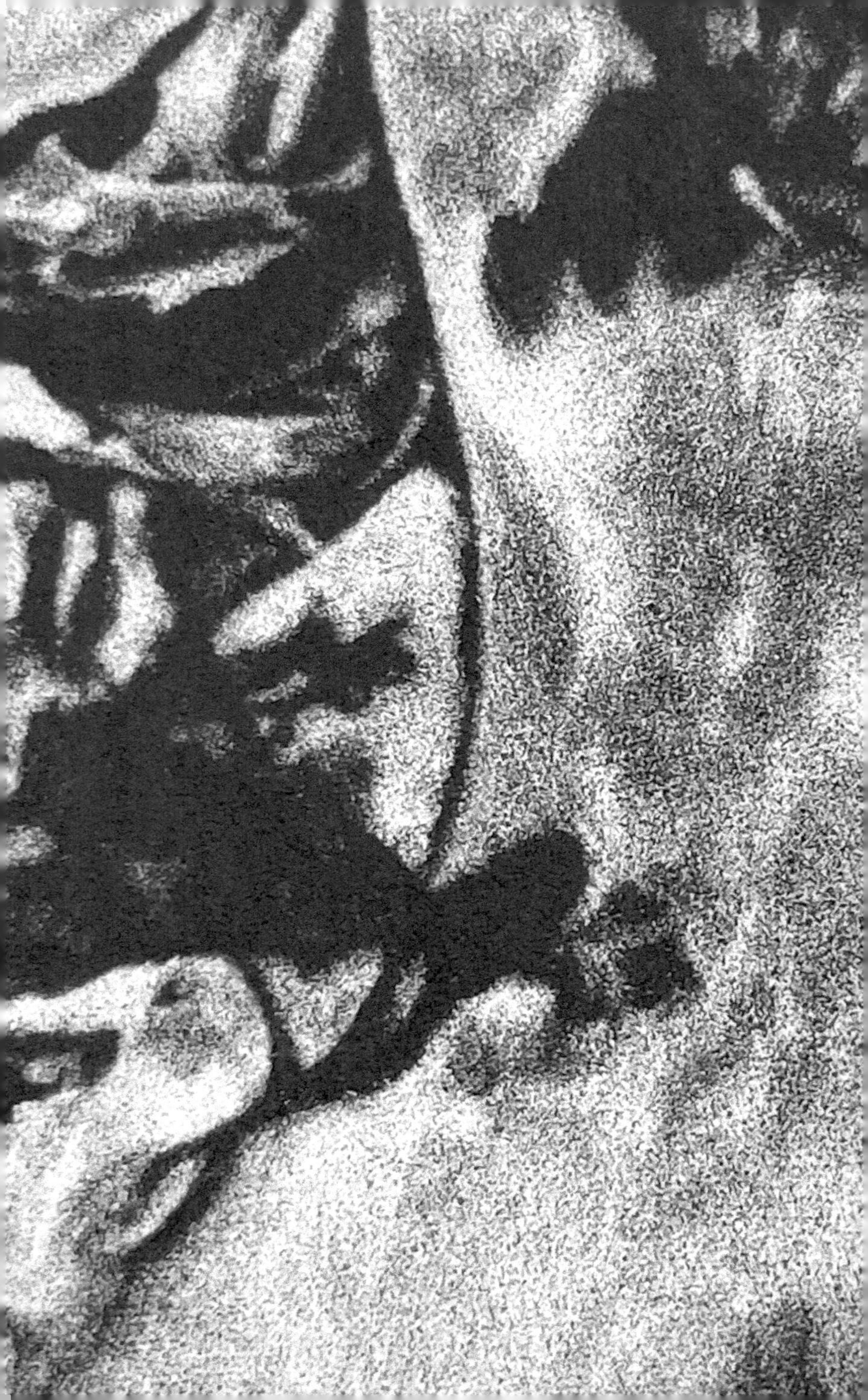

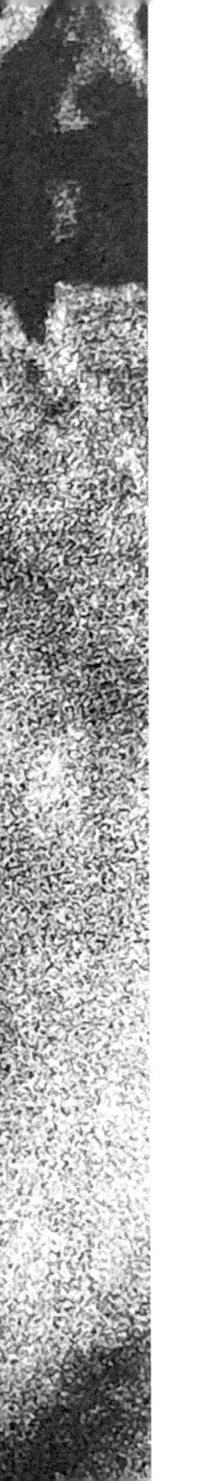

"At the genocide house
The killer is close
You can smell it"

—Alan Vega, IT

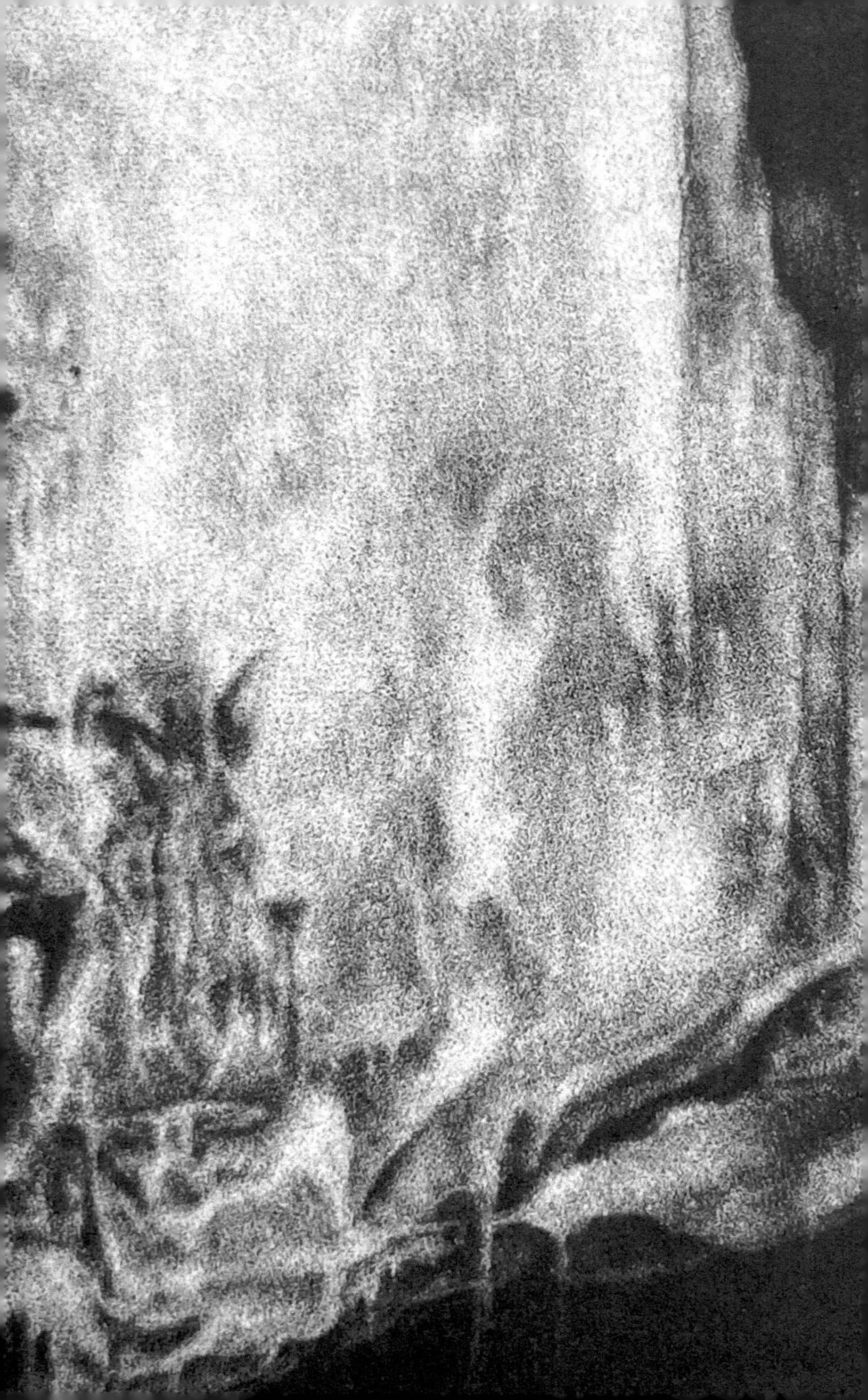

CONTENTS

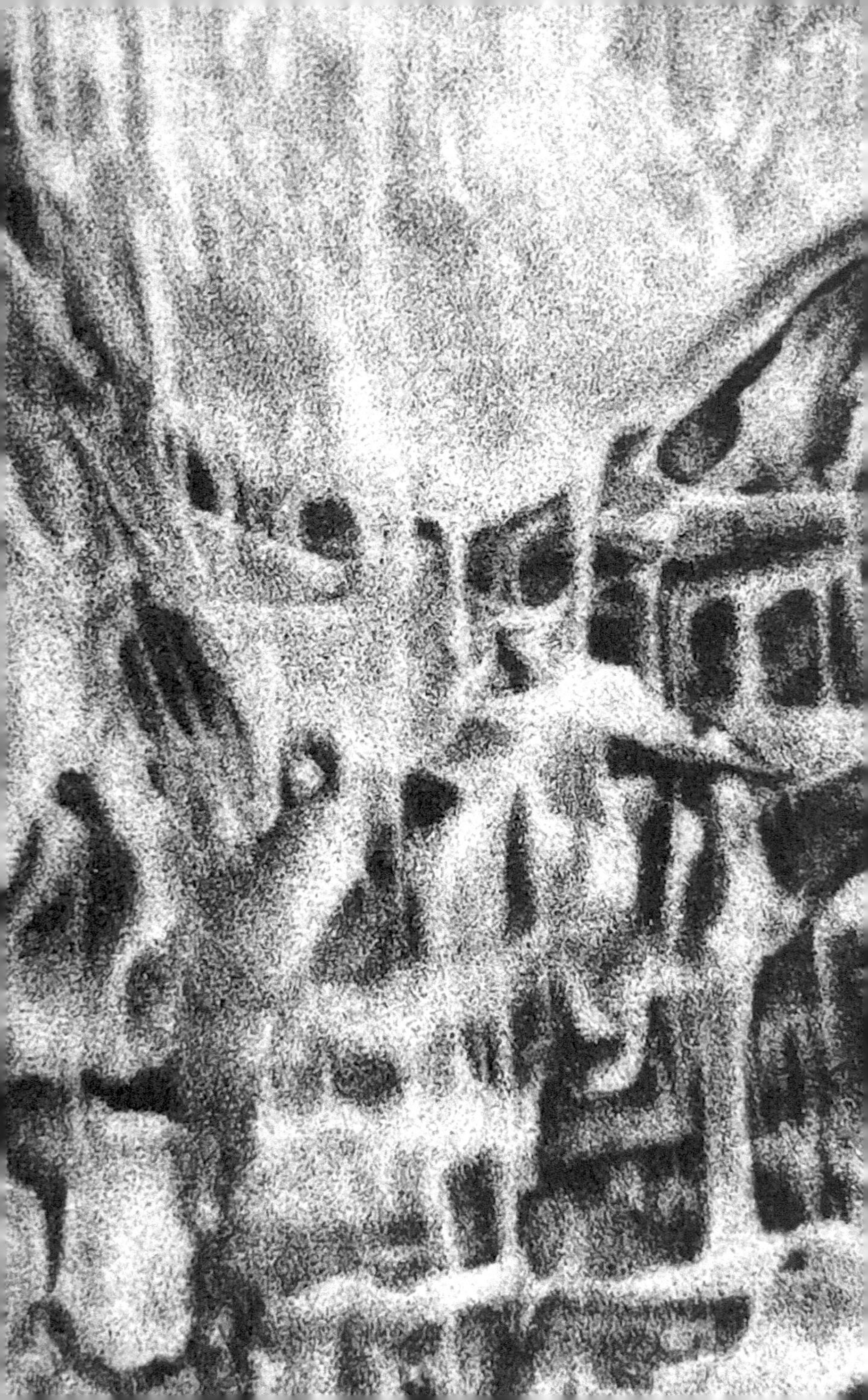

The universe—yet—not—

A city—constructed atop a city—And now atop a city—a
new city—constructed—cities atop of cities—

—many rooms—voices—peel away—Your image
reflected—smiling—Here a new skin—

Shadow worlds—truths—

Skins of bodies—the universe—
Here the dead—eternal—removed of
flesh—Here—motion—voice—

Skin—yet it is not—Sound—voice—yet it is not—

Here all versions—lives—events—variations—
transmutations—Here what was life—removed of
life—Here—life no more—

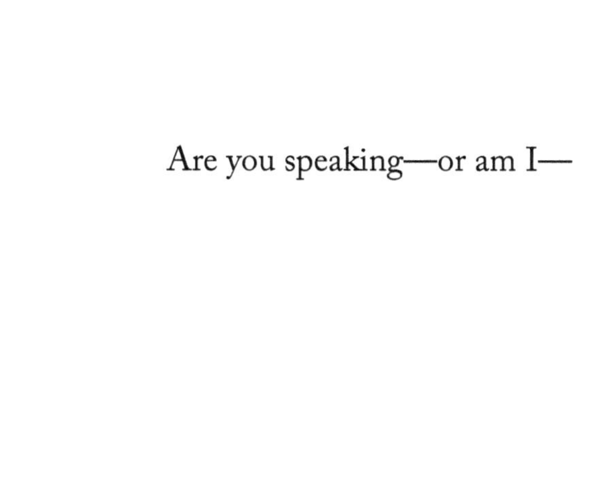

Are you speaking—or am I—

1675-1678

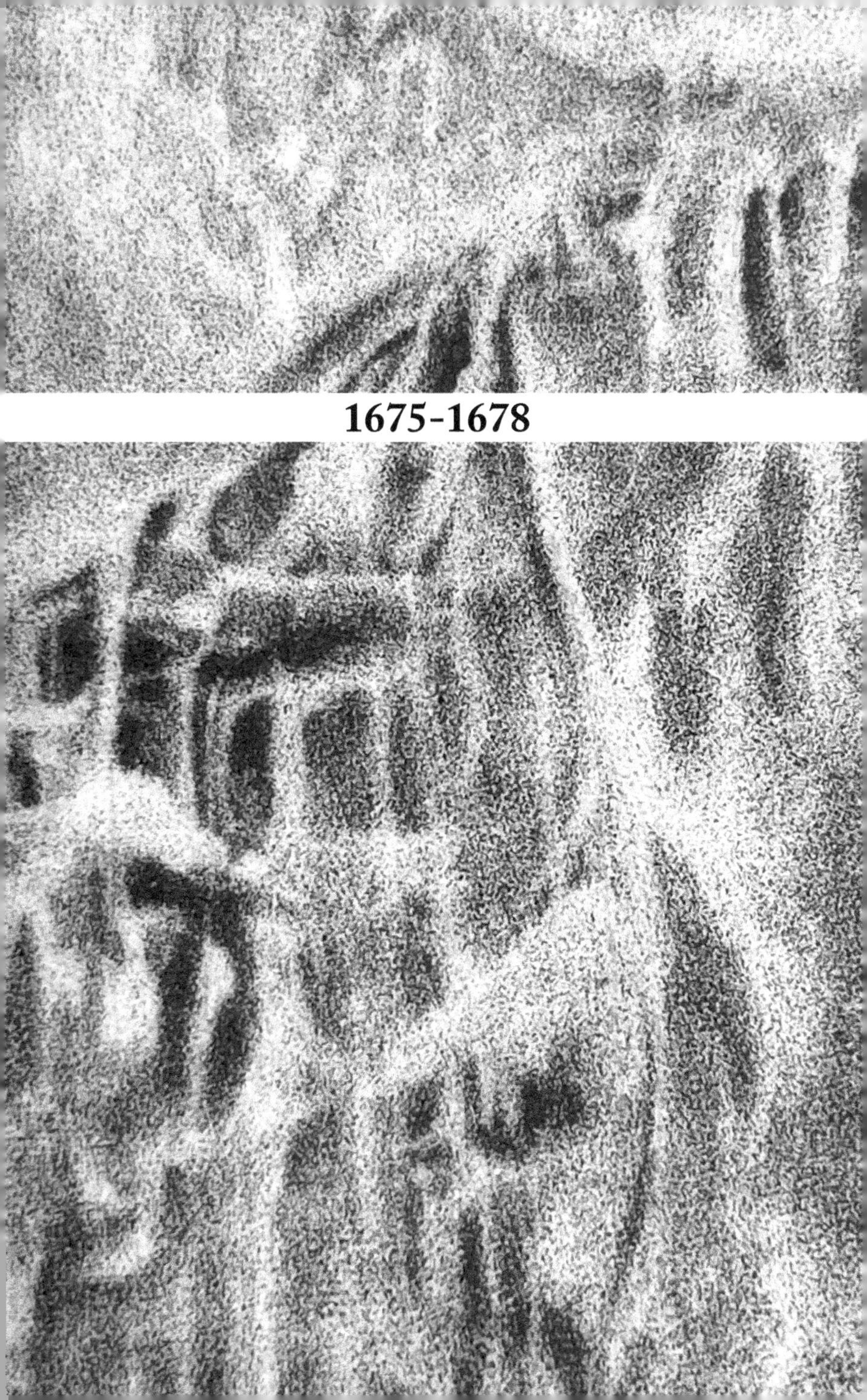

As a child—I did sometimes see the devil removing—christian bodies from consecrated ground—He had his spade— hooves and horns and tail—Black dirt and sod—over his shoulders—Carefully he pried the dead from—their womb— Their jaws—with spirit—animated—bone and—ribbons of skin—flapped—How they pleaded—Satan's mere smile—in return—

Many years since I saw him last—I have walked—churchyards moonlit—Called and called—for him—For me—he no longer comes—Now I see only his ways—

I have walked the valleys of our land—mountains—rivers— great dark forests no true christian dares enter—Gulping bogs—The heathens—thatch dwellings—dogs lie in the dirt—I have met with—mayors—the governor—Dined in their halls—faces in the candlelight—at my story astounded—To think all this splendor and horror from one mind—emerged—

Such immensity is—terrifying—

A woman alone—I think—understands—A man—with his mathematics—his electric current—and dogma—is incapable—A man in his feathered hat and ruffled collar examines a human skull and sees a skull—A woman sees there—everything—

It is astonishing so few women from these rooftops—jump—Perhaps they fear the height too mild—They lie—crippled—maimed—screaming—Such screams over many miles heard—A beast so devastated is relieved of its misery—a woman is nurtured to what they call health—Now she must account for her carelessness—Now she must blame the—frailty of nerves—She must say—I was asleep—this is how I awoke—

If not for this war—would I now in bed beside my husband lie—Sounds and shapes of our chamber—so familiar they even now seem to rise before me—No matter where I am— my familiar world—comes—I close my eyes and now in that place other—It is terrible—Would I have remained what I was—a fury—restrained—Perhaps I did always threaten— burst through the cracks—Perhaps this was inevitable—No organ or skin could contain—my true shape—

We knew so long their—approach—by heavens—sweltering—crimson—A wind of murder does come—flesh burning—from plantations mere miles distant—devastated—We have heard—stories—travelers come upon towns in flame—There is nothing left—they tell us—save—evisceration—

A cow—through a fog—wandering—the long black earth—entrails from her belly torn—dragging—

We are not so well garrisoned as those towns—my husband does say—*We will need to build high walls*—He gestures—there— *Stone*—he says—*Spikes*—Another man nods—*Yes—Yet you have seen how these heathens do climb—even the steepest fortifications—*

There is a map drawn—our settlement—the township—the dwellings—*Here we are*—he says—The further reaches— English fields—The wilderness bordering—He draws a circle—a line between us and—this darkness—Here will go our wall—he says—

The beasts would drive us into the ocean—my husband says—*if they could—*

Some roads it is said—blocked with horses—shot through their necks—hacked open—Some—of leg removed—some—their heads lifted free—thrown in this dust—The heathen in his madness does little consider the folly of this slaughter—There is no logic in his animal mind—only malice—deviousness—*The heathen*—my husband says—

My husband—his name is French yet—he is not—

Progenitor of my children—I think—He is stout—aged— He smells of—fire—labor—He is a man of prayer—When he comes to ravish me—he bids me do not move—utter no words—When I was a child he did—terrify me—Now I know to find terror in the lord—

This man before we did marry—made his will known to me—with authority—He wore the—splendid costume of his fathers—Perhaps the very clothing they wore—emerging from the forest—white trousers and jacket—blue pocket square—straw hat—blue ribbon—loafers—His legs crossed— blue stockings—His fine dwelling—there were many rooms within his house—He swung a walking stick at his side as he led me about the garden—although there was no impediment to his gait—He dabbed his throat with a handkerchief—his face reddened—*This heat*—he said—*is burdensome*—He sat me in the shade at a table his servants had prepared—cloth and umbrella and chairs—a pitcher of lemonade—glasses were filled—*Yes that hits the spot*—he said—Now little pastries—apple—cherry—cakes—were brought—*You will be mistress of all this*—he told me—gestured to the vast yard—the house—servant's dwellings—the servants themselves—

I didn't look at his servants—When they must be spoken to—I looked at my hands—twisting—

His grandfather—joined us—Venerable man—His birth year by no one remembered—Silver haired—thin skin stretched—shining—where it did not hang—In his chair he rocked—bone and vein and loose skin—a wool blanket folded across his lap—His teeth jutted from steel gums—teeth from his servants harvested—Servants no one alive remembered—In the forest they were somewhere buried—Swallowed into our lord's immensity—When the sun waned grandfather said he must return indoors—The man I would marry took his grandfather's shrunken hand—*Good night dear Grandfather*—he said—The old man did no more rise—his servants carried him seated yet in his chair—

My husband's previous wife—when I was a child—she seemed—so elegant and fine—She wore blue—her skin so pure and white—translucent to the bone—I do not dare ask about her—She remains a mystery—her manner—delights and frailties—There is nothing to know—he would say—

I know only a woman—carried forth in portrait—hanging even now in my bed chambers—I sometimes lean closer— the lamp light glows—I remember her—I a child—she a lady—How beautiful she seemed—was her hair so dark— her neck so slender—her nose—aquiline—This mark upon her cheek—Surely this was so—yet I remember nothing of it—What of her voice—this too is lost—

I have long admired you—he told me—our courtship—Carriage rides—His gloved hand—the softest leather—covered mine— He gifted me bracelets—necklaces—silk gowns—stockings—*I watched you at your father's knee*—he whispered—*Your eyes— sapphires—your skin—porcelain—your tender lips—rubies—I thought—there is a beautiful child—*

Ungown thyself—he insisted—that first night—At the edge of his bed he sat—*A woman must live in submission—if she is to live in glory*—he said—as I removed my covering—*Slowly now*—he whispered—The hearth did burn brightly yet— still I shivered—He continued—*Her submission brings her glory—even as man's glory comes from his freedom—To give yourself—without reservation—unto an authority—higher—* How I stood—trembling—in his silence—His gaze—*Come to me*—he said—his hand—a gesture subtle—

Mornings his secretary arrives—Jonathan—a heathen savage in youth made—christian—His hair trimmed to a length—civilized—Much of his beauty covered—suit of black wool—carefully brushed—his shoes—gleaming—black—His good manner—christian politeness—His hands clasped—head bowed—He shifts in place—will not even look at me—until I bid him sit—

This boy—Jonathan—no more than nineteen years— Slender—wrists and hands—Cheekbones—how lovely—if rouged—Shoulders and arms—Delicate little bird—With the servant girl alone he is abrupt—*No*—he insists—correcting her pronunciation—He demands she repeat—again—again—until finally her articulation meets his standard—*Yes*—*now you know*—he says—

How polite and meaningless our chatter—His studies—his professors—I nod as he speaks—*How fascinating it all is*—I say—He betrays no sense of his task—the room wherein he disappears with my husband—When he returns downstairs—in the late evenings—he appears half his former size—sunken—It is as if my husband does consume him—particle by particle—Indeed—how full and red—my husband is at the dinner table—Jovial—Falstaffian—Is it youth he consumes—vigor—I regard myself now—am I no more the girl I was—Fed upon and fed upon—until—a thin crone of twenty-five—

It is true I know nothing of—his life—beyond his life within this room—waiting—*There is a world to you unknown*—I sometimes fancy he will someday tell me—

How slowly time moves while he—awaits my husband's summons—Each click of the—great clock—until finally—from black boxes each no larger than—a wren's house—will come—my husband's voice—disembodied—crackling—

It is an infernal device—My husband sits within his distant room—yet his voice is here—He—assures me there is no devilment in it it—the mechanism is grounded in—principles—scientific—*Tendrils of wire*—he explains—*line the walls*—Yes—the very walls—sweltering—quivering with—electric current—Yet I am uncertain—How can mortal man possess such means—

Does Jonathan know how he groans—almost—inaudibly—at the box's first crackle—A—fearful sound—inadvertent—unmanly—Does he know how slowly he rises—the hesitation of those first steps—when my husband's voice—from black boxes—hisses—as if—steam escaping—

Jonathan—Jonathan—Jonathan—Jonathan— Where are you Jonathan—Jonathan—I will not wait a moment longer—this is madness—How it

seethes—urgent—stern—a cry—gargling—strangled—
His distant face must burst—bright—red—*Jonathan*—*I
will not tolerate this—foolishness*—Silence—now—
static—breaking—*Jonathan*—a—flat voice—void of
life—defeated—muttering—*Jonathan*—*Jonathan*—*Jonathan*—

I know not what goes on in—my husband's room—but I
believe I would rather—flee to the wilderness—than meet
such a summons—

The heathen—my husband often said—*may be trained to
the mimic the christian*—*This is true*—*Yet such mimicry is*—*a
wan approximation*—*Yes*—*there are three such savages at our
college*—*remarkable heathens*—*They seem to read*—*write*—*con-
verse*—*in the manner of christian men*—*Upon apprehending
such a savage*—*one must blink*—*to distinguish them*—*from
christians*—*then one nears*—*perceives*—*clear distinctions*—*His
attempts at articulation*—*wit*—*prayer*—

There are many such men as my husband—landowners—
farmers—men educated—who listen to him on these
matters—A man well read on the latest advancements in
European thought—German—English—French schol-
ars on the heathen problem—The various underdeveloped
species of man—Was the heathen once a man as any other—
they asked in their university corners—only to degenerate in
the forest—Was he formed on some entirely other branch
of the tree of life—

No this—literate savage—my husband said—this half thing—is a dangerous business—You have all seen—a wolf—chained—It does seem to become docile—tender—but a wolf cannot hide its derision—it grows in madness—frenzy—The native seems to assume our guise—as if to wear a christian name is to—walked draped in his skin—But it is otherwise—We believe we are—civilizing them—bringing them into light—when in truth they—drag us into their darkness—The heathen does infect us from within— By proximity—the christian is drawn into—savagery—You see already how few men on campus do attend daily service—Choose instead to—carouse—gather at ale houses—Merriment of the flesh—sinister—

You will notice how their bodies seem to perish in our proximity— civilization is devastating to their condition—You will notice how even those exceptional few—do—become diseased—incapacitated—One fellow dies choking on blood—Another walks off a rooftop—found broken necked on the cobble street—a wretched hound—laps at his blood—

My husband—by the constable called to examine—a heathen corpse—frozen—Discovered—shadowed beneath the ice— They crack open the pond and hoist him free—He wears a grey suit—leather shoes—His skin bluing and hair held fast with ice—Was this murder—suicide—They do not know— Was the heathen inebriated when he here wandered—*You see here where the ice opened*—another man said—Yes—*glazed thinly with new ice*—

Here where the hands—forearms—scrapped—torn—Perhaps— one man said—*fish—No—another—he clawed at the ice—A murdered man so thrown would not claw—said another—*My husband split the dead man's chest—*You see the lungs—*he said—*He could not have been breathing when he went under—*

*It little matters—*my husband said—He paced now before a gathering of men such as himself—in the end—*if some scoundrel murdered this heathen—or if this heathen did in drink wander onto the ice and thus plunge to his death—Or if this heathen did will his own demise—(if such an unreflecting creature may feel so consuming a melancholy—perhaps there is more to such men than we know)—Such a man could not—within this world of ours—persist—Our civilization expels him naturally—*

*The heathen is an infection—*my husband said—*You see how the infection—spreads through the blood—A limb now must be removed—*He draws a line along—*where his arm and shoulder meet—*

Before he comes to me at night he must for considerable time bathe—

Softened—yet flushed from water boiled—he stands at the foot of my bed wearing only a nightshirt—He insists—I must lie on my back—close my eyes—

Cotton to skin—How his flesh does burn—swell—within me—

He presses his hand to my throat—deeper—as if to push through—My gasping sounds—Lights—flare—sparks cascade—some divine message—sent—How exhilarating—this terror—

To bring a child into this world—I thought—is a cruelty unbearable—

By the river's edge—I watch women—swollen—undress—Gowns onto rocks—cast—How they creep—hand in hand—Toes—ankles—slowly into the water they wade—They are giggling like children—splashing each other—Soon too I'll swell—Soon too some organism within—murmuring—

All life wandereth from—the vacuum mysterious—There is nothing—and then—the first pulse electric—is this the soul—welded now to the flesh—The prison house forms—heart and vein—blood—eyes—lungs—bone—Is this you—my child—in fluid suspended—observing without understanding—a dull light through membrane—like shadows upon screens—while sounds and voices foreign—drone—From nothingness gathered—into flesh of woman—

Is this you—my darling—from my body pried—strangled—blue—What was your consciousness—a candle—snuffed—By midwife swaddled and handed to—me—sallow—blood wretched—I hold you against my breast—coo—When I force a nipple—swollen—to your lips—Your eyes—into your head—lolled—Is this you—or you no more—Has the essential element—fled—

They place you in—a casket no larger than a bread-box—Your shoulders pressed to the walls—your little feet swaddled—Your head—flopped to the left—Upon your eyelids—illustrated—a gaze unto the world—So you were captured—transubstantiation of light—bitumen—sheet of pewter—into flesh—

How quickly one is no more what one was—How quietly one becomes something—new—Is this you—Your name into slate etched—To touch the inscription—the angel, a skeleton—Is this you—under lawn—flesh—blackening—splitting—Is this you—soil and root—beetle—worm—

How he—how my husband—never again spoke of you—I did fancy his—faraway looks did signify—

A man—my husband wrote—*from christian influence removed—becomes a shriveled thing—*

In the wilderness—my husband wrote—*the soul degenerates—the light now glowing becomes a small thing—a pin prick—We have heard—a howling—These devils—I have often said—my husband said—were once men—much as you or I—a thousand generations previous—they too spoke in tongue recognizable—They too wore costumes—perhaps silken—They too—*

So my husband into the forest went—with musket—

A dozen dozen men—through swamps dismal trudged—gulping—muck—my husband wrote—Mosquitoes fat—our own blood smears—necks—palms—A constant whine—men deranged—thrashing against the air—muskets—explode the emptied air—

The cries came from trees—brush—shadows—a malevolence—shrill—They are here—a force—incomprehensible—Skulls cleaved—the body spasms—Necks spurt through—fingers desperate—Finally—a musket ball explodes one backward—his belly gulping—They are gone then—clouds of smoke and steam—

Some days a smoke—the horizon blackens—There comes a wind

of murder—

We set camp amidst the trees—my husband wrote—*fire—the
sounds of the forest alive—the silence then the crackling sounds
and an owl—there are wolves here somewhere—perhaps they will
come to us in the night—The silver moon—blotted now—darkness
complete—We sit in the awful nothing—A man clears his throat—
another spits—Some foulness does here operate—I say—In this
place the very air—does shift and warp in ways—unchristian—If
we should from the earth rise—into the atmosphere float—I would
show no surprise—*

*Sentries at camp's edge say no man has there trespassed—nei-
ther sound nor outline—At dawn—Four stakes from the earth
protrude—draped—the black hair of dead men—A mile distant—we hear first—From tall grasses—their boots—legs—We
hear the flies—pungent death—already—How sweetly lie these
christian boys in their doom—From the grasses they are lifted—
carried to our camp—carefully laid—hands across breasts—repose
respectful—We brush away the flies yet still they blacken—red
gaping heads—We shroud them—Blood wounds—into white
sheets—stamped—*

My husband's room—He alone carries the key—great and iron—from his belt it swings—A long stairway—narrow—upward into the furthest extremes of the house—the floor beneath him groans—Then there is the sound of the door opening—it does seem to exhale—Then it does behind him close—

There are days he does disappear into this room—for hours—the morning into the afternoon—

Only once did I—creep up those stairs—how carefully I tread—slowly—lightly—Perhaps inside his room he stood listening for the—slightest infraction—Perhaps he sensed my—desire to know—

Up the stairs I—creep—the narrow walls upon my—shoulders press—The humid air—my brow and throat and underarms—my belly—swelters—I lean against the wall—upward yet—an impossible distance—A line of light beneath my husband's door—How the air thickens—When a board seems to creak now I must stop in my motion—in this time I do not even breathe—How I listen—Now from his room—voices—not his own—Now from his room—song—instrumentation—a sound swelling—glorious—Human voice—sometimes—a language—foreign—Human voice stretched beyond the natural allowances of human voice—While instrumentation—rapturous—Such sounds can come only from—some god whose soul—burns and swells—a seething—boundless—exceeds the regions of his form—It is terrifying—

When my husband emerges from his room—his eyes and breathing—when he joins me in the parlor—asks of my needlework—When men do sit before him and he does carry on now of the matters of the day—the savages in their instruction—their belligerence—the crops of corn, tobacco—cattle, swine, chickens—while I listen from some room other—When he consumes venison and milk and cheese and bread in his famishment—When he drinks of ale—cider—When he believes he has emerged from his room a man as any other—returned to the world as he left it—I alone perhaps perceive what condition of exaltation persists—What glory does—transfix his earthly flesh—radiate and burn—

How my husband—his communions—secret—In his room amidst—sounds perhaps from some god thrown—prophet of the lord—privy to voices strange—A mania terrifying—There are days soon when I see him no more—when I know I must not ask—*Where have you been—I have little seen you husband—*

While I am never to his room summoned—he does beckon the servant girl—Come—his black boxes call to her—*Hurry child—* The sun does yet rise when she disappears into his room—it is high upon its arc when I next see her at her tasks—Her various positions about the room—I am—at my needlework—labor delicate—a bed rug—the tree of life—Later—this same girl—brings me a silver tray—lemon cake—sliced—*How delightful*—I say—*Yet—there is a fly—striding upon my lemon cake*—I say—How soft I make my voice—How—inviting—When finally she leans to see—She falls away—yelping—Tears—Fingers held—clasped—at her cheek—

How—I apologize to this girl—Hand her a handkerchief—even as she shrinks away—Cloth swells red—Her eyes—what terror—The slim light scar she carries thereafter—The frail story she tells my husband—a slip—fallen against the stove—

This first time I tell myself my apologies are sincere—This first time I plead forgiveness of the lord—

Evenings—a hearthlight—my needlework—the servant girl lights candles—How kindly I thank her—My husband watches from across the room—as if apprehending some—element—new and terrible—What a strange girl he must think me now—

When—no new child within me—swells—I no longer find my husband—in the night—leering from the foot of my bed—I lie awake—anyhow—What of myself am I to him offer—some devotion—What have I but my flesh—

Beneath quilt—layered—My thighs—fingers—a motion—slow—sublime—I roll onto my belly—Hips and buttocks—cadence rhythmic—while—I contemplate the servant girl—envision her called to me now—How would she taste—lips—dusky—perspiration—smoke—How would she smell—the rude wild thing—No—tonight this fantasy has little effect—I roll onto my back—my ministrations—accelerating—The arms of the blacksmith—I think—wrapping me—Brute man—uncouth—rough—No—the cobbler's apprentice—a lean bashful lad—I have seen his gaze unto me—linger—No—No—This too is—dull—unexceptional—There is a—tremendous wind—My mind through—windows—to the further world—What sin do I now contemplate—What—pleasure—perversity—denied—Somewhere in the world tonight—I think—devils—through shadows—a darkness—fluid—Now—finally—my body—radiates—with—such delight—

What separates us—living from—dead—Frail tremulous—membrane unseen—Perhaps even now—naughty spirit—my daughter—Annabelle—Thing expelled—Hovers over me—cooing—wailing—Perhaps—spirit lips at my breast—clamor—yearn—

My mother's gravestone—Sara—Her daughters—Rebekah—Patience—Susannah—blue mold—grasses thickly grown—When I was—no more than nine years aged—I tore away the weeds—pressed my ear to the ground before their stones—cool—pungent—Can you hear me—I whispered—How I strained into the darkness—Somewhere below—humming—I thought—Perhaps—groaning—

They must look as I do—or have—or will—yet—they do not—I thought—Within their caskets they must lengthen—malformed—broken—

How it must have tormented them to—hear me at my play—How they must have longed to cavort about the yard—sip lemonade—dangle string before kittens—capture butterflies—dust alive—How they must have yearned—to hold my clothing against their bodies—death smeared—To remove me from the universe—To stand in my place—sleep in my bed and assume my seat at the table before—breakfast porridge—to hear mother call them by my name—to hear mother call out—*Clara—Clara my darling—my dear—Clara—Clara—*

It is a terrible thing—to have died—and yet—continue—

It is true—I do sometimes—take my little basket into the world—raise my bonnet—Afternoon streets— November mist—dead leaves sodden—Footfalls clicking on—brickwalks—Torches already lit—for the gray hours—

So many eyes—inhaling—One senses the dead here too—yet it's the living who—

What a horror—to be observed—But I have always been watched—Who does not watch a young girl—as she grows—who does not weigh her beauty—luxuriate in her— potential—What a pretty child—She will make a—lovely woman—Who does not long to capture such youth—educate them—attire them—shape them to their—desires—until such hour they are—ripened—fit to burst—

I've never before told anyone this—but I will tell you now—

When I was a child—merely—I saw my uncle through a window—the room lighted from within—Father's broth- er—A man—goodly—church going—Stooped—he steadied himself with one hand against the wall—His trousers low- ered—pale buttocks—black hair—I had never yet seen so much hair on a body—He did not notice me—he was quite lost within his task—I could not comprehend at first—what he struggled with—

I wondered—if he saw me—would he desire my—wide—trembling—eyes—Would he beckon me in—offer to me his body—immense and strange to a child—How I longed—to explore—How dry went my mouth—How I burned at the brow—Young as I was—yet at the threshold—I did not know—yet—I knew—

Perhaps—it was the air—a musk—This is how beasts communicate—I know—yet a man—I have learned—many times over—is no more than an animal—contrary to what my husband would tell you—

My uncle came to me at night—whispered to me of—his only child—long moldering—My companion—constant—Cousin Anne—We would—with little dolls—play—*Do you remember*—he whispered—*my Annie's still face when we—laid her down in darkness*—He told me of his wife—wrapped in flame—*I will remember always her screams*—he said—

I would watch you bathe in the river—he told me—*Your pale body—hipless—legs in motion—the muscles of your—buttocks*—

I told my father once—my uncle did—speak to me in the night—*No—child*—he said—*it was a dream*—

To my uncle I might say—*Come with me—to the river's edge—green skin along—stagnant shore—Let us sit in grasses—hazy with gossamer—milk of dew—Oaks—ancient—autumnal—they wither and burn—Everywhere—miraculous smell of death—Not as you are—Uncle—so long in your grave—phantasm now—I know—I am not as I was—Yet there are others here—Young women draw up their skirts—pale bare feet—ankles—shins, even—Their family names to me—known—I have seen their faces in pews arranged—backs of heads—auburn tresses—Some girls porcine—Some—rather delicate—How dear these ones are—*

Watch them—carefully—I might say—as you would have watched me—Tell me what you—there see—

Delicate girls—vibrant—laughing—Have they no concerns—Do they not notice the—waters become—malevolent—red—Do they not hear—explosions—musket blasts—screams—echoing from towns distant—

The priests have said—there is a place—a world above this mortal perch—In some manner—it is as—this world mirrored—yet—it is not—I have been told—it is this place—perfected—

Now I believe—the true world—lies beneath this one— The face of the waters—moving—darkness—the sun through fog—burning—the trees in outline—oily—the morning mist rising—the shadow of the mist—What truth—monstrous—from us hidden—

What if I could I there travel—My arm—as if passing through—atmosphere—fogged—

There is death everywhere—Children cut down—swollen—shivering—They say it is the lord—returning them to glory—

No—the truth is he is vast—insatiable—The little ones he brings to his light—He strips them of their flesh—Their skeletons—minuscule—I might find them—collected by the shore—

In a bedchamber meagre—Shadow bodies of—learned men—
by tallowlight cast—A man lies—his final hour—His wife
pushes through—this gaggle—intellectual—The woman's
pathetic desperate ministrations—She dabs at her husband's
mouth—brow—a cloth wet—His lips glazed—sputum
bloody—His ragged wheeze—The learned men—their
remove—fascinated—*You see how the man is drowned from
within*—my husband says—indicating the fellow's throat—his
lungs—The man's eyes open—clouded—He buckles—his
arms—flail—*You see how he clings to the mortal frame*—my
husband says—*even as he is—dragged under*—

My husband's hands—to the wrist in—blood—With scal-
pel—he trims loose the lungs—wings in hands held—blood
black—sagging—

What a curious mechanism—is man—my husband says—

*You see how his body in its affliction did consume itself—How—
what was a man—becomes now some beautiful—other—Is this
the man*—he says—He pries the skull top free—with motion
practiced—removes the brain—halves and segments it—One
such piece quivering he holds between thumb and—forefinger—*Is this him*—he says—*or is the light of the man—the
man itself*—

If we remove of man his—every organ—Lungs and heart— spleen—liver—loaves of kidneys—brain—If we pull free his stomach and intestine coiled—If we render the man—organ- less—is he yet a man—If we strip him of skin—now muscle and blood and vein—Scatter him for the dogs—If we do boil the bone until he is—loose ivory alone—Remains he yet—the man itself—

Perhaps—I would say—if I knew the words—If I knew— what my husband knows—Who is to say what we call heathens are the not the true substance of the god's flesh— Who is to say my husband in his room—all the learned the men of his books—the wise men of the church—the university—Who is say they are not the—malefactor—the element—insidious—Who is to say—to drive them into the sea is not—his true will—

From a darkness—outer—they hurtle—Screaming—hollering—mocking—Bodies obscene—nude—greased—Goodly christian men before them fall—Bullet and hatchet and spear—How red the earth—a cloth foul—menstruous—Dying men—in blood wallow—choking—In their mortal hour—they crawl—to and fro—blood slop—How pale becomes a man—of soul draining—Avert my eyes—christ—I cry out—yet still I—watch—

What ecstasy—I have so long thought—to allow myself—murdered—I long considered myself sprawled—split at the belly—entrails—How flies—fat—black—upon me would dance—Knocked at the head—the white brain would spray—Seat of intelligence—yes—but the soul—I so long thought—I would not allow them drag me into their—dismal wilderness—By heathen axe rendered into—flesh of my lord—christ's goodness—christ—author of my flesh—

I did not understand myself—I thought—when the moment came—I would—

I believed I would allow myself murdered—yet when came the hour I could not—In that hour I knew only a—fleshly terror—I could not even scream—yet I ran—horror at our backs—

What a gift—I once thought—to become cleaved open—spilled—eradicated—

Yet at first cry I fled—stood garrisoned with a hundred others—Weeping—human pungency—Praying—What are your prayers to a dead god who—beats down our door—I think—Do you fools not see your prophet has returned—howling—

Heathens fall at our rifles—but it matters not for— he is infinite—Men leave to extinguish the—burning roof—They do not return—I will see them later—as if rubbish—discarded—

I thought—murder them all and leave me—I saw myself alone survived—Do not think I wouldn't have—relished my—aloneness—

It was my husband who—brought this annihilation—transposing as he did—into heathen
affairs—

If it must be murder—my husband told the men—*then there is
no question this savage met some devious end*—*You see here*—*the
flesh*—*from struggle*—*torn*—*The throat*—*here*—*bruised*—*the
neck*—*broken*—

There was a heathen witness brought before these men—
who identified the assassins—*A heathen conflict yes*—said my
husband—*but the murdered man was converted christian*—*His
murder then*—*an affront to god*—*His murder then*—*we christian
men must*—*bring*—*just recompense*—

These heathen men—hanged in the square—I did make some
show of looking away—Yet I heard clearly—deliciously—the
ropes snap taut—twist—

Now—I will explain the—long hour of my captivity—Their dwellings—quickly constructed—disassembled—Deeper into the swamps we went—at rifle shots—echoing—Smoke of fires—christians burned the forests in pursuit—

Their king—a magnificent heathen—He was aged—yet not—His savage garment scarcely covered his flesh—bronze, powerful—His english name—Phillip—Our christian meddling in—native disputes—The hanging of—innocent men—an affront unforgivable—They had no recourse but remove us from the land—

The women who tended to me—brought me plates of ven-ison—mushrooms—mash of heathen corn—Savage—yet their touch—delicate—with their infants—with me in fact—gentle always—nurturing—I must eat—drink—for the long marches to come—They did worry at my weari-ness—the hours I could only scream and weep—allow them no entrance to my dwelling—One young heathen girl holds me as if I am her—mother—or child—How tender I feel toward this one—yet—had I a dagger—

I am to Phillip led—crouched in his great dwelling—the fire before him—So near to him now I see—the lines of his age—weathering—blistering—His hair does gray—Yet the shadows shift and he is much younger—no more than my age—These savages contain—a permanence—we christians have not—

He is mortal—certainly he may be killed—yet he allows no evidence of this before me—When he speaks he does so of the ages as if he witnessed—the first breath of mist—upon ancient waters—

His son—beside him sits—Halfbreed—an abomination perhaps—yet beautiful—his blue eyes—

How quiet they are—expressions—beckoning—Phillip—a smile—faint—I begin to tell them—the information I expect— they desire—*My father*—I say—*was a wealthy man—my husband is a man of—high standing—A ransom—considerable—*

Phillip gestures for me—to quiet—*We want for nothing—what could your husband possibly give us of greater value than yourself— You would be better off remaining with us—anyway—within the year the rest of the christians will have been murdered or driven back into the sea—*

His great dwelling—cathedral of tree limbs—trunks—the smoke rises through the sunlight—He smiles—sweetly—apologetically—for the self-evidence of the statement—

I call him king—once—He insists—a king has no place within their conception—yet he cultivates an air—regal—If he says we must abandon everything with no notice—we do—If he departs for days—we await him as—the rising sun—

There are many inexplicable sights—within the wilderness—One does learn not to gasp—

In one place we find—a carriage—yet—not—a carriage—collapsed into the grasses—metal—rusting—glass and leather—They prod at the mechanism with spears—swords—

To look at it—to near—one fills with strange horror—there is no danger in the thing—yet—I tremble and I cannot stop—I do not know what it is—I am compelled to say—again and again—

Perhaps this place—to my husband—even—unknown—

In the wilderness—one stands between—a light burning—the coolest shadow—One falls into such reverie—I reach an arm far enough forward and my arm is here—no more—In my hand—a teacup perhaps—a candle—

The wilderness falls away—from a distance—leers—Before us—a hillside—fog discolored—glazed—We follow a stone road—shooting with grasses—flowers—My husband would no doubt deny—such a road through the wilderness does pass—Yet it was there—we followed it for—I know not how long—In this place—beyond—all christian measures of time—There is the sun—then there is not— Moon and constellations through the canvas glow—pallor unearthly—There is a brick wall—skin of moss—An iron gate—fallen—

We come to—a stone manor—many gabled—Some distance from the structure—we perceive only an air of woodsmoke— Nearer now—we watch—shapes of men pass before—lighted windows—Such men comprehend not what—visits them now—None can truly know—when the mysterious hand around them tightens—

The great red door stands ajar—a warm air wavers at the threshold—They anticipate us—I think—Perhaps—crouch in postures murderous—muskets—sabres—Yet Philip has many times safely traveled through—the air of murder—His existence inseparable from—the threat of oblivion—So into this manor Philip—we—the wandering tribe of Philip—went—

This manor—inhabited—yet—empty of life—Within some rooms—glass orbs suspended—flicker with light—In a dining room—a chandelier radiates—light unnatural—A table—set with silver—porcelain—beefsteaks—blood pool—asparagus—a dish of butter—glasses of wine—At the head of the table Philip sits—Of poison—he is without fear—No proxy chews his meat—it is Philip devours the beefsteak—nods—before the others divvy up the rest—

In this place—screens of glass—hang upon the walls like— silk draperies or—portraits—These are not mirrors—I think—squinting for my reflection—Curious fingers click the screens—hollow echo—Some lie mute—darkened— Other screens—flicker—glow—Yes these screens writhe with motion—Images—shimmering—They seem to depict a snowstorm—perhaps—We stand—transfixed—Now—one imagines—from the maelstrom—images coalesce—Yes—it is clearer now—Here a man—walking—Now his face— aged—weathered—fills the box—He seems to speak—*I am become*—his lips might say—*destroyer—worlds*—

How quickly this manor becomes Philip's domain—His soul stretches to every room and corner—even as he sits in a great leather chair—His eyes filling with light—the motion of screens—*Do you understand this*—he asks me—gestures to the screen—A light fills the horizon—Men shield their eyes—a cloud swelling—a terrible wind—trees—houses— swept away—The image is repeated—Now—bodies of ash—bodies—against walls—shadows of bodies—I shake my head—*I've never seen anything like this before*—Yet—I know—Yet the images follow—my thoughts—

Philip's mouth hangs open—as if a groan now—Philip now in the darkness—flickering light—

This manor—immense—foreign—Yet I could navigate the halls—with eyes closed—There are staircases to quarters— beds—musty—disused—yet the hand finds a pillow—a quilt—yet warm—Impressions there—seem to shift—A library—Phillip's son reads aloud—haltingly—*In death's dream—kingdom—these do not—appear*—I sense what he will next say—My lips begin to move—yet the words—do not follow—An orb to the wall—affixed—pulses a—white light—I reach as if to touch it—over the heat my—palm hovers—To burn alive with this—unnatural fire—radiate and glow—impossible heat—a moth—ragged—deathless—beats against the glass—my hand—

It is true—I am—a thing of substance—flesh and hair— bone—teeth—weighed to the earth—An energy seems to—lift me from my place—yet—*I am here*—no place other— Here is the proof—Before a mirror—a basin—a spout—a steady drip of water into cupped hands—spread over my face—Soap—pale—blackened in my hands—

Here is the proof—Any common butcher or butch- er's apprentice—or heathen savage—Any—attendant to a—slaughter—We who have seen—the carcass—split open—understand—the soul—radiant—perpetual—fas- tened to—a doomed animal—Here I am—I thought—flesh stretched over bone—Bone atop organ—assembled— Organs—artery—vein—Now comes—our decay—I thought—

Now—our decay—How the vessel—atrophies—the membrane—thins—hangs—Hair once auburn—black— becomes—gray—The floors rattle with our teeth—fallen—We shuffle along—stooped—Philip too—perched in his leather chair—hoary—shriveled—The screens—His eyes—clouded

with images—flickering—men marching—men—naked—
emaciated—men—dead—piled atop each other in—great
pits—A hand passes before Philip and he—knows it not—

How long in this manor—There comes a groaning—One
speaks and cannot hear their own voice—Perhaps the structure itself—means to devour us—Who can say what such
a place—wants—

Yet—none of this is real—

Yet I know—none of it was real—After we depart—it is as if we were
never there—A place once magnificent—recedes and recedes until it
is—gone—

Yet is not the very tissue of the world more mysterious than we suppose—
Perhaps many devils wander the wilderness—phantasms—shadows—in
and out of substance—lesser versions of our dead god—

A   bear   headless—on   hind   legs   stands—claw-
ing a tree—In gesture—futile—to consume some life
within—We keep our distance—the men circle—motion us further
away—without themselves nearing—They could shoot it and—shoot
it—still it would stand—quilled—a hundred arrows—fluttering
from its hide—Somewhere yet—the head does lie—moaning—

Other scenes of wickedness—follow—

A heathen man cuts his own throat—We find him—against a tree—drained of life—He was smiling—laughing—when I last saw him—They leave him where he lies—Crows and foxes will come—A heathen woman—lost to the river—I alone saw her leap—She did not scream until she was—by the current—swallowed—A pit—human skeletons—a hundred perhaps—entangled—Steam—from the earth—scarred—gapping—A fire—gusts—The air—trembles—bends—Grasses wilt—A tree—ignites—

One dawn Phillip will leave—the other men—They go into the wilderness to murder—pillage—*It is a terrible task*—Phillip says—*We take no pleasure in eradicating your people*—Yet—note—how he smiles when he speaks—

His son remains—follows me on my walks to the river—helps me fill skins with water—The grasses these mornings are frosted and his breath escapes in white mist—He wears only a garment of buckskin—yet he betrays no sense of cold—How glad he is— to finally speak his mother's tongue with someone other than his father—I do not ask how his mother perished—it is all the same—How carefully he articulates her name—*Sara*—as if felt within his mouth this first time—He watches my reaction—*Did you know her*—he finally asks—He knows only—she was long ago taken from a village such as mine—I shake my head—*It is impossible to say*—I insist—

His mother—Abducted undoubtedly—christian from birth—Her devotion to eternity—the lord—annihilated by the wilderness—What must her soul have felt—in this—darkness—transformed—

When again we meet—will my husband even know my name—Or will he look upon me—bewildered—*Who are you*—When again we—I will greet him—a mystery—in new skin—draped—My soul—will burn—He will know me not—I will see through to his organs—bone—marrow—I will see every particle—He believes—to cut open a man upon a table is—a revelation—No—he sees nothing—compared to what I will see— When the men return—ears from their necks—strung—boasting of how many christians killed—farms burned—cattle—mutilated—None of their heathen number ever seems diminished—

They have captives—christian—women—weeping— meek—They have watched children—slaughtered—against rocks—dashed—What kinship am I meant to feel toward them—Their homes—treasures—marauded—burned— Most in their horror do not speak—respond—when I place before them—meat—corn—Some chew—distantly—Their eyes—vacant—lonesome—*It is not so terrible*—I say—Other times I insist—*We will be rescued—My husband will pay our ransom*—

What of theirs remains—Have these women any home—family—Their husbands decay in some forest—anonymous—Even their dead god in this hour—No—What reason have they to live—Am I so sinful—To hear their wails—and feel only disgust—disdain—When came this corruption into my soul—It was not only the heathen—At first light—pulled into this world—a child—unblemished—would I have wept for these women then—

Alone at night—my dwelling—seems to expand—cavernous—the roof to the stars extends—Scrapes that place where the lord must drift—His light touches me not—I feel only the soil—

Some god perhaps beneath the soil does move—I think I do sometimes feel him below—

How vast the wilderness is at night—Incomprehensible—Noises—alien—one's mind must meet the void or become—devoured—

I almost laugh to envision myself as I once was—wandering about this place—I in my little bonnet—my plain simple dress—my basket—A lighted torch to fend off the dark—How long before creatures from the darkness onto me leapt—their teeth—claws—rend—clamor—How the hot blood spills—The woman I was before could not have contemplated such—ravishment—Being—torn—dismembered—conscious of my obliteration—I would not have known to arch my back at the thought—clasp tight my thighs—rock in motion to—screams—echoing—How exquisite my terror would have been—I can almost taste it now—a mouth brimming with blood—

I cannot know what I would have thought then—How incomprehensible this old self seems—freed as I am of my—Clara skin—

I could never have thought—much less to my husband said—*Darling lay me upon your table*—I could not have directed him to take his fine little knives—pleaded—*Open me—please—open me—you must—*

Outside our camp—within the forest dark—Heathen prisoners—bound at wrist and ankle—They wear our—christian garments—brass buttons—stockings—leather belts—boots—Jonathan—I long to cry out—He must see me—yet he shows no recognition—

For Jonathan alone—I cannot sleep—He is—sweet— tender—He is not—these other men—He alone would I protect—cover with warm blankets in the night—

Did he too carry a rifle at my husband's command—unfurl maps across some table—makeshift—Did he tremble to kill—

For Jonathan alone—I appeal to Phillip—*He is a—goodly man—gentle—docile—He carries no malice within his heart—*Phillip smiles—as I speak—massages between his thumb and forefinger—a christian woman's ear—blood blackened—*Yet into the wilderness he went*—says Phillip—

For him alone I would—creep into some captive woman's dwelling—Such a woman in her terror—might not—even struggle—How pathetically she might mew as I—remove her garments—*Quiet you*—I will hiss in her ear—If she begins to bray I will take a rock to her skull—

As a woman—gowned—Jonathan will sit before me—My neither this—nor that—

You were never that man they saw—now you are that man no more—I brush her hair from her eyes—How long we will allow it grow—How fine and lovely she will look—*I am your sister now*—I tell him—*Your true sister*—

Together we will lie down in the weeds—our secret voices—in this wilderness—united—

Our days together—when we are—to the civilized world returned—Our every fancy shared—Books of poems together read—We take tea—I bid Jonathan whisper of her—various amors—men she has married in—ceremonies secret—*What is the marriage bed for two men*—I will ask—*Describe for me—the manner of the union*—How she will answer while I brush her hair—slow strokes—Weave braids—luxuriant—

Into town we go—hand in hand—our minds—united—We give into our—little impulses—What they call sinful— Shops—ribbons—fabrics—how lovely a garment we could—Chocolates shared—we giggle like children—Daily beside me on church pew—We must pray to this god—yet someday—perhaps not—

It seems there is no place I could not go now—having seen the world—high and low—

Together we will visit a tavern—what secret rooms therein— Smoke—thick—musicians—In this place—men no more appear as men—powdered—rouged—gowned—ornate—So too—Jonathan is gowned—wild flowers in her hair—while what spare whiskers once—to the skin—shaven clean— *How beautiful you are*—I tell her—*What man would not want such a bride*—Enough delusion—Even a child understands—there is no reprieve in this world—Little agonies—terrors—miniscule—Between trees a web—dew glowing——a fly—devoured of life—Worms from the earth struggle forth—Drowned in rains—they lie pale—sodden—A fox—a husk—spills with maggots—Where single soul once house—now—made plentiful in death—

The heathens form a ring around captive men—to each other bound—Silhouetted by fires—heathen men step forward— jabbing spears into their captives—bludgeoning them with mallets—The heathen crowd—cheer and dance with each blow—There is no atrocity they do not relish—

The heathen captives—buckle in agony yet—they remain stoic—Jonathan alone wails—*This is fiendish*—I say—*No*—Phillip insists—*This is our gift to them*—

You must watch—Phillip tells me—*I am*—I say—I do not look away now—How easily one watches once—given permission—One feels the old hesitation—drain away—Jonathan—I think—could I have gone in your place—harden myself—I would allow myself not a grimace—not a sound—

You are weeping—Phillip says—*No*—I say—

In the wilderness there is no reprieve from the darkness—
The stars loom ever—Even in the daylight one feels the
universe in motion unseen around us—a dead god's soul
outstretched burning—a million lights—

Through forests and swamps we trudge with urgency—ever
greater—Rifle shots—echoing nearer each day—We wake
coughing—the fires christian men set in our wake—They
are coming to free me—I think—

How clearly one sees the nearing—obscenity—They will
slaughter every last heathen man—make servants of the
women—clothe and house the children—educate them—
They will burn every final tree of wilderness—build upon
the carcass—farms and dwellings—churches—while—ever
more christian souls—chanting and bowing and singing—
How quickly they proliferate—They will need to build cities
atop of cities to house them all—A million little rooms by
candles lighted—

What will they do with all the dead—the bones will burst
from the ground—They will pile them in attics—house
them in chambers—The buildings themselves—from bones
constructed—Cities entire devoted to nothingness—

They will return me to civilization—Jonathan's bones—a
burlap sack—at my feet—My husband in his—military

finery—seated across from me—Carriage jolting—while his medals—wag and clang—He does not remove his hat—red plume against—carriage ceiling—bent—

Already they are erecting new structures atop the ashes—

Other women once captured are now—returned to their houses—husbands—Some already round with—new child—We chat in shops—our bonnets—christian cheer—Fingers pass casually over—fabrics—candies—baubles—So many more delightful baubles already than before—Glowing—shimmering—What temptation—What vanity—displayed—as if they know the things their dead god once told them matter no more—Soon this city will become—a city of baubles—This dim woman before me—brought to the same wild as I—yet—she seems untouched—I search her eyes while she—talks of what inanities I cannot guess—silly lips—thin gray lines—I see only her expression—depthless—

What they call the world—is a skin—only—thin—lacerated—puckering—Through the membrane—shadows—move—I press against the—folds and scars—I think—Here is an opening!—and here!—Nobody—save for me—sees how easily one may—push through—

Phillip alone escaped into the further wild—Devils weave him into their fabric—

They will never find him—I thought—He was already transfigured—the forest substance—Phillip—become the trees and moss—the river—silver light and sun reflected—Become the fish—gulping mouths—Become the swaying weeds fish feed upon—flecks of insects—drowned—Become—murder transcendent—pervasive—constant—Putrification—bone and hide of muskrat—fox—beaver—the gutless flapping corpse of fish—skin and skull and scale—Become—green filth collected—vile egg—spillingfree—Fornication—richobscenity—succulent—thrusting and shuddering—gasping—merging—Phillip—become the wild—Phillip—become—everything—

Yet I will find him—in every crevice—every—fallen tree—splintered—rotten—Somehow I prefer him here—to know he knows—my every footfall through dead leaves—my every breath—

Ripe berries—dusty—fragrant—burst—tart—moisten—my fingertips—my lips—I slurp the river water—from pale palms cupped—my hands ruddy while I drink and drink—My husband would cast me out if he knew my heart—Is this sin—I do not care—

I am at my darning when my husband tells me—Phillip is found—Slowly I say—*He is dead then*—*Oh yes*—my husband nods—Even more slowly now—I ask—*Did they find him—hanging from a tree*—He seems to flinch—almost imperceptibly—astounded perhaps such an idea could enter my mind—Now—he squints looking at me—How quiet he is—leaning forward—closer—as if he does not sit across the room from me—as if the closer he comes—deeper into my mind—

No—they dragged him from the earth like a squirming rat—The swamps around him—burned—My husband says—They discovered—tunnels through the earth—They set fires at one end—and waited at the other—Perhaps they called him King while—

O Phillip—you spill across the grasses—A man—transcendent—timeless and bodiless—made man again only so they can murder you—To your knees collapsed—you who knelt for no one—coughing—tearing your throat—Your eyes weep—for the smoke alone—A man made less than man—a man kicked and bludgeoned—stabbed—gouged—A man made—flapping meat and shattered bone—dirt and bruise—spittle—blood—

They suspend his corpse in the city square—his limbs outstretched—with rope drawn—The weird silence of the corpse in place of scream—Even were he alive he would not scream—I think—

My husband brings me to that place where Phillip's head on a pike—stands—blackening—tongueless and eyeless—*What do you think of your lover*—he says—I do not answer—*Do not look down*—he tells me—lifts my chin with his hand—*A terrible waste of a specimen*—he says—*yet there is value in such displays*—There are many cracks in what I call the world—fissures—I am in that place beyond all places—

There is a room—I realize now—in the ether—for us each—

Within this room we—

This final day—My husband summons me—to his room—You're ready now—he tells me—Upon the walls—depictions—illustrations—I think—shining with sunlight—There are dozens of them—Hundreds—perhaps—Many no larger than the palm of my hand—None no larger than the page of a book—*Look closer*—he tells me—To them I walk—How I tremble—I am almost overcome—He steadies me—*Closer*—he says—Now I see them—clearly—How shocking they are—indecent— The same woman is—depicted in each—She is—wearing black lace—Her—legs—belly—breasts—uncovered— She is bound to chairs—beds—poles—What remarkable work—These illustrations seem formed with—the very essence of life—*Who is the artist*—I finally ask—*Nobody knows*—he whispers—*They were painted by no mortal hand*—

Now I see her face—eyes—Why—she could be—my very reflection—

—while a funnel of smoke before me rises—If it wore a mouth it would speak in a voice—familiar—

I don't understand—is all I say—

1886-1894

The sky is rent with wires—It is no wonder a man cannot think—The city is—whispering—locust sounds—No wonder I dream a stranger's voice—One cranes one's neck and sees the sun—lacerated—drawn open—A wire can be pulled taut—and through—a man's neck—before it is impeded by the spine—while the vital fluid—sprays the walls—even the ceiling—

—a mechanism—horseless—will—

They will butcher horses in the streets—hack open their necks—shoot them between the eyes—blood melts the snow and—meat piles—steaming—There are moments—wherein one perceives their fate—

Perhaps—For so long I believed this the—sound of my voice—

Are you the man come to bring oblivion—

Did a dead god dream you—open a mouth crimson and you climbed free—

It is true—I no longer sleep for when I close my eyes a—vision singular—appears—A room much like this room—Yet it is not—

Through windows—an illume—No, lightless—

Somewhere in this room stand—bodies—shadows—perhaps—They speak—There are moments in this room—I know I am not myself—For—years—I have watched them—enter our gate—come a thousand miles to tour our facilities—Men—bearded—freshly shaven—suits—watchchains—bankers—speculators—doctors—politicians— Schoolmarms—children—

They perceive clouds of smoke—the fumes blacken—They cover their noses with handkerchiefs—I have watched men vomit at the smell—There is no shame—it is a natural reaction to an air of—

Of course the air is pungent—moist with blood and shit—lard burning—It is true, what they say—the rivers have run red—bubbled with fat and offal—

—rushed to slaughter—there is a beauty in the confused parade—The hogs—delicate brutes—are cooled first—boys rub their flanks with chilled water—for fear of a—meat fevered—

Do they know—Every motion—alien and strange—the very air—fecund with murder—

The killing floor itself—you see here the world made new—the mechanical liberation of life from flesh—the spirit flees in terror—spews forth in the blood—7500 hogs a day—We must take great care—the slightest bruise will devalue the meat—

Here a boychild fastens the chain to the hog's ankle—the wheel turns—What awful motion—a three hundred pound hog torn from the ground—screaming—The sticker's easy movement—like a machine himself—within a vast mechanical organism—and the blood is freed—torrents spray—

The hog is no more—already the wheel progresses—a new hog screams—darkness then—and again—and again—The constant tide—of scream and flesh—tide of beast split in twain—viscera removed—clumps of gut and organ—glistening—

—boychildren sweep blood clots—sawdust—meatfilth—into gutters—

The hog sticker punctures—punctures—Slopped in blood—gore—It loses all meaning—These are motions he carries out in his sleep—There is only the task—He and his fellows—a thousand in unison—They do not slow until it is all dead—

he body itself—the sacred human body—its cock and tongue and fingers—heartbeat and lungs—is no more than a mechanism of fluid and atom—a machine constructed by a dead god to—murder and shit—to create murder devices to set his task more leisurely—

—the more we murder—the more we must create—Flesh grown from other flesh—come and blood—microbes—congealing and blossoming—The fruit moans into the world—slick with filth and skin—wild matted hair—The thing itself is blind—totters—Eyes and veins—teeth—brutish—dullwitted—They outnumber us by the millions—

How quickly we brutalize them into nothing—how quickly they revive—

It continues—even in the still night—even in a universe silent and asleep—The creatures—perhaps their souls—spirits—spasming—shitting and baying—The shriek of awareness—and some—rough dead sound—a mallet punishes a skull—groaning chains—The mechanism proceeds—

There are moments—when one's destiny does—

Clara alone is here—

I discovered you—I tell her—In the Exchange Building she sat—one woman amidst a thousand—their typing machines—stiff mechanical clatter—*I pulled you from the filth*—I say—

It is not a courtship—something far more momentous holds us together—

Come—I told her one afternoon—*I will show you the floor*— That first day—we did not yet speak openly—I did not yet say—*If only we could freeze the moment when the spirit flees— Its eyes—the flesh itself—when a hog becomes a carcass—and yet not*—

I did not yet say—*We live in a place beyond their screams—yet we long to—dwell within*—

They sound almost human—she said—and she did not look away—No I have never seen her not in command—

She once told me she is from St. Louis—the daughter of a pharmacist—She fled on a steamship—smoke—Men—their hats—rumpled suits—linen—Ladies at the railing—Vagrants—wandering the waters—I close my eyes—Clara—a child amidst the sickened—panorama—*Were you terrified*—I ask—*Terror is*—she began and then—*I could no more bear them*—was all she would say—Another day she tells me she was—married in Texas—A burnt land—cattle—the skulls of cattle—He was a rancher perhaps—*Where is this husband now*—I ask—*What if I said I killed him*—*Was he a drunk*—I ask—*a lout*—*Would that make it better*—I shrug—*Perhaps*—Slowly she continues—*What if I told you he was a kind man*—*timid*—*Gave children sweets*—*wept to see a deer shot*—*and opened*—*What if I told you I cut his throat while he slept*—*out of pity*—*disgust*—

We were not yet open—exposed—when—

I came here because of death—Clara wrote—*The air—seems curdled—putrid—*

Her hand falls onto my lap—I remove it—*I will be your lover*—she whispers—I say nothing—I do not even look at her—My throat is full of blood—heat—How she laughs— Perhaps she believes she has shocked me—Later she will insist the wine got the better of her—But I will remember she had no wine—

I am not always here—I tell myself—*I am not always myself*—

There is a man who speaks for me—walks—Who carries out my tasks—instructs underlings—At night he slips into my skull—swells into my skin—

No—*I am not myself*—*I am not here*—

Clara alone is—crouched in my velvet chair—Her great book of appointments and tasks—

She is saying something I cannot hear—Perhaps the anarchists have finally come to kill us—

Now the barber tilts me back—His mustache waxed and—white vest—soap and brush—razor and—How slender he is—assured—To Clara he speaks pleasantly—*A storm later today—perhaps*—he says—His lips red—bright—blood to the surface—swelled—I watch him speak—his tongue and teeth—How warm his breath—Beneath his apron—one cannot tell—perhaps unclothed he—I close my eyes—How easily he could split me open—

There are rooms where meat hangs spread like wings—

Some men long to wander—amidst a thousand carcasses—suspended against decay—They have never seen anything—so grand—

In this city I have built—I sometimes think—time—the body—do not function as they should—

I have made something new of it all—

If not for Clara I would never leave—She is always costuming me in some manner or other—Dress coat and black tie—for the theater—dinners—in the light of day—Short coat and top hat perhaps—the museum—Perhaps a thousand years from now we too—our great works and skulls—The city square and market—carrots—chickens—The vile human swarm—They say Chicago is a city alive—thriving—The future—I see only those death has not yet assaulted—ludicrous—the universe will soon blot them out—Perhaps we attend a ballet now—she leans to me—whispers—She finds it beautiful—No it is foul—obscene—I want to scream—Fill the room with ether—and bolt the doors—I thrust my fist into my mouth—bite until the blood—There is laughter somewhere—O god it is monstrous—

If not for her—Anything I need exists already in the yards—meat and wine—barbers and soap—doctors—tinctures—sweet ether—pills—

Blacken the windows—I will say—*I don't care how*—*Blinds are not enough*—*See how the sun seeps through*—

Tar the windows—I cry—*the fumes will drive my fever*—My hand barely visible before my eyes—A sofa burning for a torch—A haze throttles the world—

A thousand years hence they might pry my carcass free—leatherbrown—hollowed of organ—Tack me to some university wall—*A hideous specimen*—they might say—*How many do you think he killed*—Clara tells me—The family she was born into—swollen with—brothers and sisters—a cousin perhaps—her parents both—a grandmother—

The old woman called them by the names of her dead—Her grandfather killed in the revolution—a ball tore his arm off—Bled out in a cornfield—*Yet she saw him in my father's face*—Clara said—At all hours she wandered from the house—They found her in the public park—staring at the trees—They found her ankle deep in mud—before the river—Perhaps she would have drowned in waters—gray and foaming—Her body discovered a dozen miles later—by fish consumed—a woman no more—Instead—the attic room they locked her in—*How easily one is forgotten in the darkness—I was to feed her—lantern light—spoon by spoon—milk—broth—porridge—I made her jaw to chew—Sang her little songs one sings to an infant—The rag doll I brought her—she cradled now to her breast—Her blue eyes dimmed—her chin—the frail white whiskers—The body decays I thought and hair trembles forth like—a potato sprouted—I longed to pluck them*—Clara said—*but the old woman screamed*—

She'd forgotten how to speak—She believed the shadows upon the walls—the world itself—I pressed my ear to the attic door—her moans and cries—I was only 11 or 12 but I thought—

When I was a child—a very young child—she held me—whispered to me I was a pretty girl—It was cruel to not kill her then—Clara said—

Did you want to—I do not ask Clara—*Did the attic have a window*—I could have said—*they would have found her tangled in a bush—*

—a pillow—I did not say—*an old woman can only struggle so long—no one suspects a child—In the morning the windows are opened—Already the clamor below—*

Each day our city becomes ever more infested with life—I tell Clara—*The degraded races here congeal—Germans—Swedes—Poles—*

I have no sense for their language—strange, guttural—No, I understand them not—

Their wooden homes—Window to window—trousers, shirts, gowns from lines suspended—ghostly white—buckling in the wind—Children in rags—boots and hats—crouch watching—soot—bricks—dust of bricks—wagon tracks in mud—mud alleyways—

Lovely older boys—their ragged trousers held up by fingers through loopholes crooked—sulking in the ruin—

—cabbages fester—newspapers with blood—strewn—shit and slop—

The young man upon his cot—his hair matted—blistered lips—he is wheezing yet—His friend stands in the corner—his coat and hat and the wind rocking through the window-panes—How his eyes glow—In the doorway—a wretched mother and infant suckling—In the alleyway—perhaps the father—a shape halffrozen—blue—the frost pale alleyway dirt—eyes swollen—his lips—

Another room—the little girl—Perhaps 12—14—Even she does not know—Cadaverous—her sunken eyes and cheeks—bones of wrist and arm—Soot and rags—Her belly is swollen—She tells me her family sleeps on the same straw pallet—While the others slept—her father—perhaps her brother—She tells me it is impossible to know—They are so alike at night—pulling her closer—

If not for you—I do not tell Clara—*I would drink carbolic acid*—
They will find me in my own shit and piss—*a husk swollen*—*They
must not preserve me*—I do not tell Clara—Even as a carcass—
pickled or smoked—I want—no more this—tedium—Theaters
and opera houses—Hotels—gold leaf—marble—Corinthian
columns—Hot and cold water of course—Elevators of such
speed—cafes and shops—saloons—*It will be the greatest city in
the world*—I have said—How unrelenting—the days followed
by more days—It is all the same—Someday—What wind
drones through streets—timber laden—A howl—devours
us—*Finally*—I thought—*nothing will remain*—

There are many rooms—only I have seen—Windowless yet—children lie—blue in the moonlight—Limbs tangled—bone tears through—blood black—Some faces—a mouth—toothless—Soon—the eyes too—Boys—smutty faced—pouty—lewd—I have seen them in the war—masquerading as men—frail mustaches as if—pencil etched—They too may kill—some are shot through the neck—I have crouched to watch—their mouths bubble—Others—the arm explodes—

There is no such thing as innocence—I have thought—ants and flies make their nests—I will build such a tower—I thought—mold and slime and bone—*None but I may look upon—A child swollen*—I begin telling Clara—while she—washes my brow—a cold cloth—

The doctor brings—His lamp of glass—and inside a sponge—soaked—*Breathe deeply*—he says—Now the vapor until—

Finally again—the languor—*I am here*—I said—*possessed of my full senses—I could stand if I wanted to—I could read any text you place in front of me—My dear doctor you could stab me now and I would feel nothing—*

My body rings as if—a bell struck—

I will tear my mind open—I do not say—*until the dead god stands before me—I will recognize it is him for he alone knows my name—*

If I were a man—Clara whispers—If I sheer my hair—bind my breasts—But not too stout—manly—No I abhor the word—The concept is—foul—I prefer—a man—she says—yet not a man— My perfume and frock coat—embellished—a pocket square—a cravat—My buttonhole—a lily—My boots of—patent leather—

She covers my eyes—there in the darkness—she stands—

What would you do with me—she asks—Would you peel me open—Tender—hairless and lithe—My—lips—asshole—My neither this nor that—Would I drive you mad—

If not for Clara—I would never leave—In the carriage— Clara's cigarettes—the blue perfumed smoke—Now the Palmer—hotel saloon—here boys dart with telegrams— Travelers—men of business—esteemed so-called—spitting tobacco—their ceaseless money yammer—A fellow stumbles to us—drunk although it is not yet noon—He brays—*What an astonishing city this is*—Beside us—the urchin we acquired on the street—a rough lad—Clara opens her cigarette tin for him—The waiter brings the boy whiskey and soda—The child—regards us warily—He tells us his name is Samuel— later—he does not respond when I so address him—He is a cunning animal—I thought—Soon his thin vulgar mouth— slurs—His pale cheeks—blood ruddied—Now we feed him—whiskey alone—Clara takes his hand—*Such a lovely boy*—she tells him—He does not pull away—His eyes— loll—*I agree*—I say—*I own this building*—I tell him—*and many others like it—There are rooms only I have seen—But I will show you—*

If you were a lovely boy—I tell Clara—slowly without pause—*I would lock you in a room—furnished with only a mattress of straw—At night—by the light of a candle—I would watch your body—rise and fall—listening until—The anxiety—burns and swells—Beautiful lad—*

Hips—slight—the smooth bones—your rosey—Your face so still it might never again move—

I have always found the sex impulse a curse—I tell her—*In animals it is as if a madness overtakes them—you have seen it—For me it is the same—The seed burns and burns—until it is—expunged—*

This room—a table and white cloth—places set for three—The boy's mouth—fat with steak—his plate pooled—a fluid—pink—I have so long considered this moment—perhaps it has already happened—

How he flails—thin mews—sputter—*Hold him fast*—I tell Clara—Black blood—clots her hair—the table cloth—swollen red—The very atmosphere—sopping with iron—I too—this baptism—

Don't let him close his eyes—I shout—Her voice somewhere— How long I have awaited this moment—I gaze and gaze until there is nothing more—

I follow him through the thicket—Dead grass and—This brute—I thought—wild stink and heat—How many men has he murdered—rebel women chased down in fields—The months have ravaged him—Dysentery and the droning empty hours—But I see what he was—Ruddy neck—pale body—muscle knotted—dense black hair—How he would pummel me into the mud I thought—

Yet some days—I do not leave—Perhaps I allow Clara bring a tray—The stench—nauseates—ham—fat dappled—eggs—a sauce—crimson—This tedium—cutting and chewing—This show fascination—*Yes quite good*—I might say—Even in solitude there are tasks—one cannot avoid—the body will not permit it—What is man but a mechanism—shackled to its organs—constructed to consume—expunge—Perhaps I allow a lamp lit—Perhaps—Clara may speak of the weather I cannot see—No—I can bear only silence—No some days even Clara must not enter—She calls to me through the door—*Are you unwell—Shall I bring the doctor—laudanum*—Her voice is—a knife through my skull—*Leave me alone*—I whisper from my great velvet chair—*No more*—

There are too many people—I do not tell Clara—*Too many eyes*—*Their voices*—*sniveling sounds*—*How can they tolerate their own thoughts*—*I do not understand a man who has not longed for*—*annihilation*—I do not tell Clara—*I believed the war would*—*cull the herd*—*We left them bayonet cleaved*—*rib bone and entrails*—*Others*—*as if angels dreaming*—*lips flowered*—*red*—*You are better this way*—*I whispered to them*—*We burned Atlanta to nothingness*—*Women and children fled*—*weeping and sooty*—*a caravan sluggish*—*We should have followed on horseback*—I do not tell Clara—*Bayonets*—*I do not say*—*Our bare hands*—

Leave—I tell Clara—Never again enter this room—The boy—sprawled—He is beautiful—flowered—his eyes yet—spread—With my fingers—now my tongue—I touch his cheek—His lips—of salt and iron—

I pull him to the wall by the wrists—How immovable his new weight—The bones wrench free but the skin holds—

How quiet he lies—slumped—I could reach into his throat—to my wrist—now the elbow—My body entire—

Even now he is—transforming—none but I can bear what he will become—

Soon no scrubbing will remove his stain—

Had I been killed in the war—cloud of blood and earth—what was my arm—scattered—bone splinter—Surgeons flung arms and legs from hospital windows—heap of meat and flies—Perhaps I lie tangled there—

My father—Clara says—wrote home—between marches—Swamps—fields—Tents—malaise—We read his first letters—aloud—Winter evenings—candle light—Mother wept behind—a door closed—

Then—we heard no more—Clara says—Lincoln was shot and dead—and buried—yet—of Father—nothing—The thought of him moldering—anonymous—a skull to be discovered and displayed in a thousand years—like a Roman vase—

Perhaps—he fled—Men disappeared in such ways—I say—For all you know he is—living in—Texas somewhere—California—No—she laughs—Not that man—

Perhaps—I also lie—in a morass sweltering—limbs and flies—The increasing dead—thrown from carts—

Can a man persist in two places—even if in one he does—molder and decay—

There was—a boy—Beautiful child—When asked his age he replied—eighteen—But I knew him no more than fifteen—He had—a fine high voice not yet turned—So he sweetly sang Lorena—Home Sweet Home—while some one other played a fiddle—a banjo—

When he did attempt—coarsen his voice—shadow his features with—dirt and ash—I said—*No lad you are lovely as you are*—I dipped my fingers in the river and washed clean his lip—cheeks—

Did he ask—*Lie down in the darkness beside me*—the forest floor—musk of rot—stagnant waters yonder—

My arms about him—tender nape of neck—ears—sun blistered—

I watched you—across the fire—Boastful—lewd—How you did love to kill and fuck—Drink oh be joyful until you could no more stand—and the others laughed—Ah beauty—mascot adored—*I'll carry him to his tent*—I insist—*Let him sleep under the stars*—they say—*it will teach the boy temperance*—How they laugh—Do I later creep to you—a fire light dying—the vast universe above—Do I crouch to watch the dew gather like sweet pearls upon your throat—Softly snoring—fragile lips trembling—How deeply you sleep—even on fields of annihilation—Child—I do not ask—What restless violence compelled you—across towns and prairies—A hundred miles trod—your blistered feet—boots no more than rags of leather—You slept in ditches—fled wandering dogs—Your father will see you nevermore—your mother—

On field of combat—a rebel stranger—anonymous—yet you had known him many years—Every motion between you seemed—a memory relived—You swooped beneath his charge—His belly—you rent beautifully with your bayonet—a blackened flower there—How he lay—from the mouth bubbling—His eyes—as if inflated—A terror serene—Now your bayonet tip to—his Adam's apple—Perhaps he would burst—You have already been here—All of this is known—

—rebel women—thrown to the lawn—breathless—weeping—A widow in black—frenzied spitting—The fellow atop her was laughing—*Hold still Missus—hold still goddamn you*—A slave girl screaming ran past—A solider carried a chicken in each hand by necks broken—How wide your yellow smile since the terror began—*Save some for me boys*—you yell—Swiftly almost hunched you trotted across the lawn—so I followed you into the house—Union boys—opening closet doors and flipping mattresses—an attic door was opened and up the ladder they disappeared—You were in the pantry—to your wrist in peach pie—a handful dripping to your mouth— Now you threw open cabinets—*Where do these Rebs keep their fucking whiskey—*

Had I known myself then—I would have remained in the house burning—outspread on the widow's canopy'd bed—The ceiling and walls—must swelter—a blackness—glow and throb—and burst with smoke—noxious fume—The house seethed and moaned—while the air—the essence living—was devoured—The building collapsed—and still it consumed—I alone remained—saw things in the maelstrom no living man may see—

I will burn—yet I will not—The pain will drive me mad—but it will mean nothing—Don't you understand I cannot be destroyed—

*When I found you—sweet child—in the Wilderness burn-
ing—Even—face down—I knew—for none were so small as
you—*

Cherubim—your throat cleaved open—crimson and bone—

*I would remove—your guts and heart—wretched instruments—
needed no more—You are pure now—*I whispered—*a new
thing—*

*By now child—you are—charcoal and ash—the loam of a new
Wilderness—You stand before me—wretched vapor—Wander my
hallways—When you speak—Your lovely voice—lost—within
the vastness—*

Blacken the windows—I tell Clara—*We will carry candles*—*I dream the sun blotted*—*eternally*—

Clara—yellowed—a haze—*Perhaps I was the one who murdered you*—I tell her—*Perhaps*—*it was some man who followed you home*—

Is a shade cursed to know what it is—I cannot remember—

A dead god floats somewhere in the ether—He has dreamed this already—

When war again—*from the ancient vastness*—*rears*—I tell Clara—*You will ride beside me*—*gowned in mail*—

We will hunt the anarchists—*drag them from their beds*—*screaming*—

I will open them for the crows—*How beautiful our city*—*their organs glimmer like*—*fine jewels*—*the intestines for a crown*—

*They will call you Saint—a Saint of Murder—I tell
Clara—Patron Saint of Terror—*

My lovely saint—I whisper—My—neither this nor that—You alone did not flinch when the swine was stuck—removed of organ and pried apart—You alone—did lean forward to—better see—

There are rooms—I alone may enter—Yet—when you close your eyes—perhaps you see what is there—

Chamber sacred—A floor crimson—Alter of—hair and bone—The eye socket hollow—teeth—

*You woke—screaming—*Clara said*—Eyes wild even when quieted—*

*I dreamed a light—*I said*—a cloud—rising from—where once a city—I have watched many cities burn—the dead—the wandering near dead—This was different—There was a light—now where once a city—ash everywhere fell—A girl child to me from the flames—burning—screaming—*I thought*—I wrestled her to the ground within a blanket—Beneath my weight—crushing into ash—Now I too—blistering peeling—*

The wind—as you know—carries extinction on its breath—

There is no more beautiful organism than war—a great cloud—colored—sulphur and blood—some men within—are singing—

I close my eyes and I am lost in it—There are laws—I do not tell Clara—but there are not—War alone—is above god—

Two men alone in a tent may love each other—It is—a brotherhood—sweet, tender—Together we wake—His lips—a nectar sublime—He reads aloud his letter home—He tells his wife he believes he will soon die—

From his window—he looks out over the yard—scurrying bodies—Races—degraded—he says—Clara wrote—The Teutonic and Pole—the Slav—are adequate butchers—proficient with cleavers—mallets—Covered in blood and flies—Your Englishman—would vomit—but the Irishman—No—One sees how dull their eyes—They come here—Why—he asks—smiles—Why does a louse ride a dog's back—he answers himself—

Soon we will know real darkness—he insists—Not this—low haze—Finally then—no light will penetrate—

His shadow in candle light—his footfalls—pacing—His— breathing—Clara wrote—He refuses the laudanum—My mind burns—he cries out—

I take his dictation—by candle light—

My dear Mayor Harrison—he insists I write—We were vapor once—eternal—tracing the face of the water—

When he sleeps he dreams of blood—When his mouth opens—

My dear Mayor—the god who did rule this universe floats dead in the vastness—Some cloven god other rules this earth—The first man and woman—indistinguishable—raised from his shit—

The anarchist louse—he tells me to write—The anarchist plague—You see already—the infection they carry—

Mayor—

A male anarchist—a female—It matters not—I would burn their dwellings—cut them down as they scurry forth—Their offspring—I would smear its brains on the street—

—only a weak man—fails to exterminate a louse—

You cannot know what it is like—to live as his instrument—he tells me—Clara wrote—

I have thrown myself from this window—a hundred times—I have thought—Now it is finished—No—a cloven god—seizes me—mid plummet—Now I stand—without blemish—

His cruelty is immeasurable—

Mayor—Is not every moment of goodness and pleasure a—precursor to affliction—

My dear Mayor—

His he-goat's head—woman's breasts—His cock—obsidian—shining

How voluptuous our god is—my—dear—

He pisses upon alters—and whispers beneath doors—I will tear apart—he cries—I will join together—

I give them everything they desire—a good scrubbing—a little blood does pink the water—attire them—wool trousers—linen blouses—Dapper—they turn before the mirror—winking at themselves—

I would gown the prettiest—Paint their faces—But these boys will have none of it while they yet live—

They have never seen such rooms—wall tapestries hang— maroon—gold—The carved ceiling—phantasms in combat—A chandelier—lighted—In—tongues mongrel—they marvel—

I give them wine—split pea soup—lamb with mint sauce— boiled potatoes—Ruddy your cheeks—I say—*plump your lovely bellies*—

I fasted—forty days and nights—he tells me—Clara wrote—
My body withered—skin—bone—organs thrummed through
my skin—the blood—

His fist—membraned with blood—Clara wrote—

*The servant girl brings a tray—tea—little cakes—*Clara wrote—*The police swine—thank her—*

*How busy you gentlemen must be—I say—*Clara wrote—*The world—unmoored—These anarchists after all—Explosions—a red glow—A woman—on the street—scattered—blood and brick—glass—Her infant—The papers don't describe the infant—I say—*Clara wrote—*Perhaps you gentlemen could—elaborate—*

They sip their tea—smile respectfully—They again ask to see him—I apologize—Only I may open this door—I insist—And only I may enter—

*There is a room—he tells me—*Clara wrote—*only he may enter—Here his boys will live—until—Here they will sit— eat—drink—They will become pale—larval—Hanging upon the walls—portraits painted by the long dead—their amusements and fascinations—Their progeny—infants swaddled—bear the faces of ancient men—Male and female child—gowned—without distinction—Pet cats—hunched— simian—A parakeet—A squirrel—caged—Here a garden—a tiger—a bear—A man nude—his genitals infinitesimal—a woman at his feet—suppliant—*

A young boy in this room reared will soon know only the souls of dead painters—His own voice—echoing and echo- ing—Save when to him I speak—This is the history of our wars—I will say—This is how many were killed—How they were—stripped—mounded in ditches—The child will hear nothing—

Some nights they are here—he says—I watch them from my great chair—Swine—sheep—throats gaping—skulls—pulverized—They have no eyes—only wounds—tongueless mouths—teeth caked with blood—

Yet they mill—eat potted plants—

One becomes—sentimental in their age—he says—I cluck my tongue—call to them by name—They hear me not—I clap the louder—Perhaps blood clogs their ears—

They wake me at all hours—baying—chewing—Ah— lovely brute—he coos toward the floor—holds out a hand—beckoning—Where did you come from—

*How frantic his eyes—*Clara wrote*—You bolted the doors—did you not—he asks me—the windows—*

*Did I finally kill you—he asks—*Clara wrote*—Is that why you are here—*

I found my god there—cloven—You will be no more what you were—they told me—You will become what you have ever been—They drew a line—from my brow to groin and now— skin sloughed to ground—Sheathed in man no more—they said—*This is the true thing—Blood—sinew—bone—crimson draped—*

*He closes his eyes—*Clara wrote—*He can barely speak—yet—still he whispers—indicates absent areas of the room—*

You see how beautiful he is—a young boy—into manhood ripening—How pungent—Every orifice and pore—a musk—blooms—

His cock swollen—purple—red—He offers it to me—No lad—I say—He reaches for my own—Just sit—I tell him—I want only to observe—I tell him to defile himself—You foul child—loathsome boy—

There are rooms—where we could marry—You the groom and I your maid—my gown and veil—In those rooms I am something else—In those rooms they call me by a new name—

*Bind him to his chair—he tells me—*Clara wrote—*Perfume him—rose water—Shave him—chest and arms—underarms—groin and ass—Rub him with ointment—make him glisten—Yes see how he shines—*

There is a whip in the cabinet—You will lash him until you can no more lift your arm—and then you will open his neck—

*His condition is ideal—soon though he will sour—He is here—yet he is not—*Clara wrote—*I will build a tower—he tells me—Wonder of the world—none but I may look upon—Lovely boys—into ivory boiled—femur—sternum—pelvis—gathered—together strung—arranged—Skulls outward—a stare vacuous—Yet I know them each—cherubs they were—Where once sweet lips—my fingers trace a—smoothness eternal—I forget nothing—every scar and pock—Every moan—scream—How they taste—salt and filth—dead skin—dirt—How they scamper away—hairless, blushing—Their cocks—nubile—a nectar—viscous—How their eyes flash—when they know—Too quickly then—the flesh—cools—stiffens—How I—pry open—lips and teeth—He shows me his fingers as if they—bear some mark—There is no mark—I tell myself—*Clara wrote—

I assure you he is—incapable of harming anyone—Clara wrote—

He fears the devil—He hears what he calls whispers—He believes his soul endangered—

It's true—He does lose himself sometimes—

He's forgetful—His hands beat against his face—his eyes— He stares at me from his—velvet chair—I could cleave you in half—he tells me—They would never find you—

No matter—I have heard it all before—

*He rose from bed—*Clara wrote*—I could only scream—*

He was unclothed—at first I could not understand—his abdo-men—legs—groin—torn—bleeding—His bedsheets—blood black—

You see how voluptuous I have become—he said—the true thing at last—

He tells me he was once—shot through the throat—You see here the scar—

You are blessed—I whispered—My hand onto his—clammy—so weak it seems a child's—

Some dead god other—he murmurs—from his tomb in the vast-ness—conspired against the vacuum—took dust in hand and blew—Now the atoms writhed in terror—from the universe burst green shoots—mosses trembling—

Life is malignant—you see how necessary murder becomes—

*When he desires summon me in the night—Clara wrote—
he presses a button—now my quarters flare with light—a
ringing—more and more I believe—he does not sleep—*

*—then came the fever—spasms—His teeth will break—I cry
to the maid—Now he lies—unmoving—entombed until—*

*Twice each day we must strip and burn his bedsheets—wretched
with fluids—He lies in his stench—unknowing—It breaks my
heart—You cannot understand his genius—I tell the maid—
This city would not exist—You would not exist—without this
man—Yes madam—she whispers—We work wordlessly—our
breathing—heavy—He murmurs—Phantoms—a world of
corpses—Don't listen to him—I tell her—She is discrete—well
compensated—Finally he takes the laudanum—Finally—he
lies—silent—his mouth a fish's—*

*He lies rotting—*Clara wrote—*Bone and vein—Skin—transparent—What hair there was—we remove now in clumps—Toothless—human no more—yet he speaks—I know you did this—He tries to grip my hand—*

What did you use—strychnine—arsenic—cyanide—aconite—It will not work—There is nothing I have not attempted—

We will remove the organs—he says—as they perish—I will tell you how—

Did this happen—Did he bring me before a furnace—glowing—He stoops to—a mound of coal—No—Fingers trace black teeth—Ah sweet youth—he whispers—

Did he ask—Can we not preserve them—arrange them as they were in life—Create some mechanism to give them voice—Before a great table—they sit anew—perpetual—yammering—

The fruits and meats we do furnish—gather flies—molder—Our boys care not—

*I must go—he tells me—*Clara wrote—*Yes of course I say—I dab his brow—He does not attempt to rise—He murmurs of a western place—There his god awaits—*

A famished land—a circle in the dust around me drawn—Occasionally—a lizard—a tongue flashes—A scorpion—crimson—ventures to the circle's edge—it will not enter—

Why have you journeyed to this place—it asks—*I have come to murder devils*—I say—*He will devour you*—the scorpion says—

I become—sun withered—a corpse Egyptian—During the day—I bury myself in dust and the dust blisters—At night I lie shivering—*If I could die*—I think—*this cold would kill me*—

A horizon burning—dust swirls—a flash—distant lightning—

He leads a—bleached horse—bone and tendon—I have never seen anything more terrible—He has no eyes—shrunken pits—yet still he perceives—

He will say—*Eat of me*—His arm scorched tastes of— roast lamb—Drink of me—His breast to suckle—Milk of sin—Milk of life perpetual—

I want to scream but—the vastness hears nothing—

Interlude: 1969

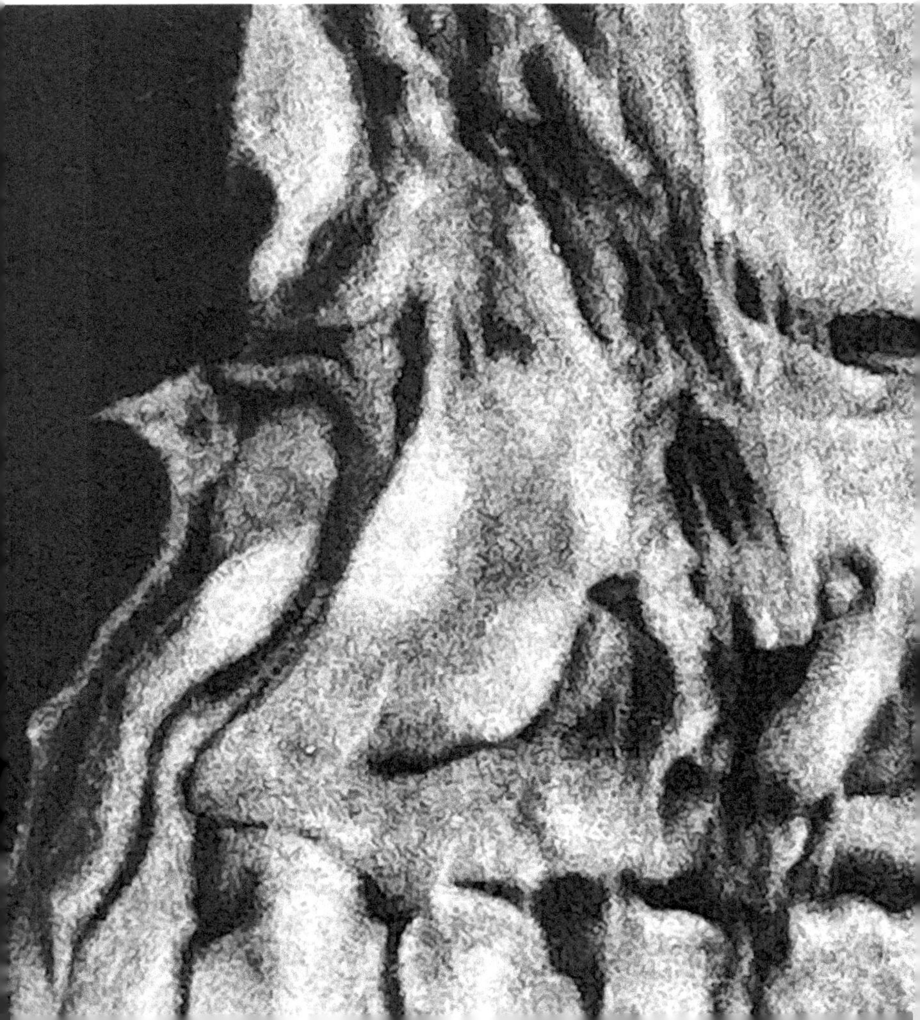

Here—the living—the dead—eternal—motion—voice—

Three men—Depictions—replications—ubiquitous—posable figurines—cereal boxes—billboards—magazines—the front covers—shoulder to shoulder—smiling—blue eyed—stout shouldered—addressed within—every mundane fact—height—weight—birthdate—favorite—book, animal, color, food—

Commander—Neil Armstrong—Command Module Pilot—Michael Collins—Lunar Module Pilot—Edwin "Buzz" Aldwin Jr.—encased in—draped with—nylon—rubberized nylon—Nomex—Mylar—Chromel-R—Plexiglas—polycarbonate—

The—sun—god—a canister—into the void—shot—

School teachers—newscasters—chart their progress—The vastness they traverse is—not emptiness—space is—light—dust—ice—stone—metal—what is called—matter—forces unseen save by—theory—mathematics—philosophy—

Skin—flesh—yet it is not—Sound—voice—yet it is not—

Listen—

Whispering—crackling—There is an odor—one said—of buttermilk—soured—

Hey—we've got a fire—in the cockpit—one says—We've got—a bad fire—We're burning up—[inaudible]—Then screams—then—nothing—

—pure oxygen—consumed—carbon monoxide—they were surely—already dead—asphyxiated—when the flames—

—video—black and white—fragmentary—bursts of static—what seem to be—corpses— slumped—tangled—smoldered—hairless—their spacesuits—melted—scorched—

SPECIAL REPORT—There was a flash—and that was it—They died—silently—swiftly—

Through telescopes—from rooftops—we may observe—black dot perpetual—passing nightly before the—face of the moon—There will be no mission of retrieval—

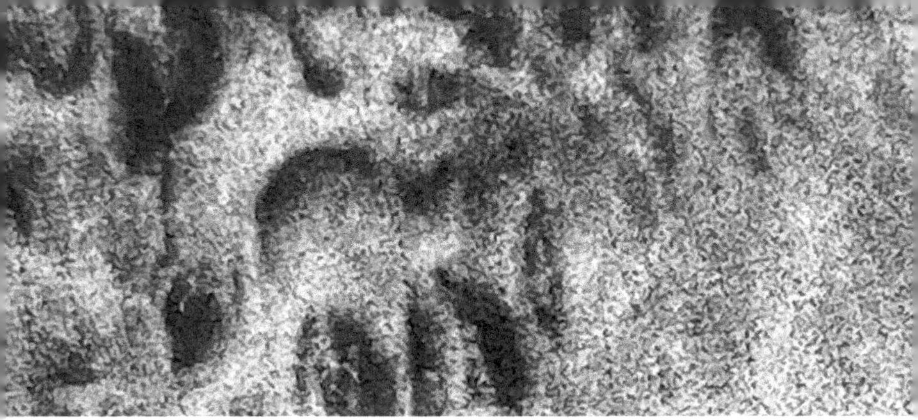

1918-1921

These are days of rapture—

Darkened theaters—Fotoplays—evening performances—Matinees—The newsreel—a woman—mink coat—pearls—the man beside her—gray hair—top hat—doughboys hustle past—a steel worker's strike—a gray haze—wires—smoke stacks blurred—cops watching the crowds—Charlie Chaplin—his latest romp—Mr. Douglas Fairbanks—his most accomplished—Maurice Tournear in "The Broken Butterfly"—H.B. Warner—"A Fugitive From Matrimony"—Sometimes you doze off—gray light swirling overhead—Sometimes you can put your feet up—Somedays you leave—suddenly—choking back—screams—The silence—immense—the silver light—

You receive letters—The sender claims you are her cousin—*Dick*—she writes—*I know you are alive—Dick—I was so afraid—I imagined—whenever I read—the newspaper headlines—I saw you killed—a thousand ways—Dick—I know you're alive—But I can't forget what I imagined—*

How angry I was—she wrote—when you enlisted—this vile war—immoral—idiotic—You thought you were being selfless—You weren't—You said they would draft you anyway—There are always ways out—You were their fool—

There are other letters—wandering—fragmentary—musing—
These letters—expect no reply—These letters—a voice into
darkness intoned—

The world—is everywhere—

—the chasm—opening—The sudden waking—wild terror—the breath that will not come—

The sky—vessels drift—a shape mysterious—the city blackens and a siren wails—Newspaper photographs—white light of flame in darkness—Husks of apartment buildings—walls removed to heaps of brick—dust and scorch—If you squint—a child's hand—pale in the ruin—Spotlights in the night—

—the vast ruin—world abyss—Men unimpeded by an understanding of or a desire to know what force compels them—into wire and gas—explosive and bullet—A man legless brays for his mother—His friend shoots him in the head—Exhilaration—A joy of slaughter after weeks mundane—The smallness of life after this—Men torn into rubble—bleeding and screaming and crawling until the charge punishes them into the mud—World fracture—Horses—maggot swollen—into putrescence swallowed—A man—faceless—yet still he screams—

The sky drawn open—blistered—Machines crawl across the sky—beetles upon a screen—Machines spiral—flare into light—Shadows—onto buildings—cast—

Yellow fog crawling—Faces insectile—Horses screaming—milky eyes—intestines thrown—Bodies ghastly—wrapped in sheets like larvae cocooned—

—a voice disembodied—*We have no quarrel with the hun masses—Exterminate the tyrants*—

—city streets—brass bands in tumult—batons—noise patriotic—Now the flag hoisted—weeping and smiling and cheering and shouting—Men wearing straw hats give speeches through bull horns—*Extermination*—someone cries—*Slaughter*—Street children—newsboys—beat each other in alleyways—a child naked, his neck—bruised—yellow and red—discovered in tall grasses—some say his genitals were removed—Eradication—a man brays—Stray dogs—mangy—snarling—

—the louse—blood thick—Emperor of—

—a million dead—heaped—Tangled in postures unnatural—necks broken—shoulders dislocated—Oozing—with flies—Some smile—yellow and green and blacken—Open eyes—bulging and tongue hanging—gazing over rooftops—

The world—wire barbed—the world—noxious—screaming

and groaning—machines whistling and spiraling—chuffing smoke—

The world—How many thousands die—The seemingly healthy—into fever—vomiting blood—The dead pile—rotting—heaped in gymnasiums—empty lots—

A twelve year old boy—discarded at the intersection of—Nude—bound at the wrists and ankles—gagged—covered in dried blood—He had been castrated—

A package lands—ticking—before a little girl—she is blown apart—her mother—thrown against a tree—

A man—murders his wife—his two daughters—himself—finally—with arsenic—When they are found—the door barricaded with furniture—hacked open with an axe—The windows bolted shut—sealed with tar—

A window wrenched open—a man—long—lanky—pale—dark haired—steps through—shoes shining—His teeth—bones discolored—yellow—

A little girl discovered—at lake's edge—She is nude—bruised

at that throat—blackening—wrapped in mud—weed—from
her mouth a crayfish—crawls—

You pass under a great stone archway—Here—a city within a city—hotels—restaurants—taverns—telegraph offices—

Here—the air heavy with—blood—shit—

The man who hires you—Mr. Thompson—bald—rotund—fought in the Spanish American War—*The fucking mosquitoes*—he said—*were like fists*—You nod—say nothing of France—vast trenches and wire—How relieved you are when he does not ask of it—You say only—what relief you felt when finally you saw the statue upon your return—her torch—robe—verdigris otherworldly—

You sweat in the summer air—beneath thick denim pants—leather boots—You wear—leather gloves—leather apron—swing a mallet—Great black and brown and white steers—noses dripping—their eyes—straining—bulging—They too smell blood—

—a steer's legs—drifting overhead—unconscious—what dreams—a meadow—perhaps—some memory residual—a world previous to man's first impulse to cultivate—herd—slaughter—Another man—beneath—a knife into the creature's throat—a torrent—sickening—into gutters—tanks—It becomes fertilizer—There is no inch of the beast not rendered into some usable—sellable—product—

Drained of blood—head removed—legs broken—stomach opened—skinned—tail removed— intestines—Stone floors collect—blood—meat—fat—Removed of hide—halved—ragged edges trimmed—Rapidly—it rolls along—Become now the subject of the butcher—

Outside—the city—shuffling—gnawing—braying—Automobiles—smoke—gases—Noxious city—screaming and groaning—machines overhead—whistling—spiraling—a white vapor—trails—Alleyways—cats yowling—screeching—Garbage cans overspilled—refuse heaped—Milk—grease—lard—flies—blood—cream—cockroaches—rinds—maggots—bones—raw flesh—shells—ivory peels—fat—fish heads—skin—curdling smells—

This city—a world unto itself—every manner of race—preoccupation—proclivity—

Buildings—piled atop—buildings—Tenement shacks—became—tenement structures—stone—brick—laundry strung—window to window—women leaning out windows—shouting—men—naked from the waist up—smoking on fire escapes—Alleyways—yards—ofslop—piss—shit—Lankwretched dogs wander—Children—smoking—sooty faced—shouting expletives—This gives way to a bazaar—commotion—rows of card tables—Endless wares—Shouting—leaning—leering—scowling—proprietors—long graying beards—faded derbies—kaftans—

Men are robbed here—beaten—murdered—Vendors—bearded—crouched on stools—sausages—hot dogs—intestines pale—raised—from steel cauldrons—dripping—steaming—laid onto rolls split—mustard slathered—You are famished—you devour it quickly—rubbery—pungent—Fruit stands—bakeries—Shoe strings—fine carpets—wool suits—gowns—trout—perch—duck—prairie chicken—snipe—milk—butter—eggs—

Thompson—His long pale face—his office—glass—steel—wood—papers—filing cabinets—He laughs—light overhead—yellow—the flies in the heat—his neck tie—loosened—He is telling you—*I can see you get it—I could tell from the start*—He tapped his brow—*Sharp*—he said—*you're sharp*—He is telling you about his grandfather—*He practically built this city—This was just a—fucking swamp—No city—a country village—a cluster of shacks—there was nothing—He was there when they started putting planks down—He was just a kid—bone saw in hand—His boots in the slop—*

Tour groups—visit this—city unto itself—*The yard remains*—the guide said—*the fascination of the world—Even in the midst of world cataclysm—*

Our process is the most controlled—humane—in the history of the world—There is precision in his movement—not merely force—he must strike—just so—When done correctly—there is no suffering— The tour guide indicates you—awaiting the next steer—You notice them not—Your ears—throat—thick with blood—You see only—the moment to come—

There is no more efficient operation—Henry Ford himself gapes in admiration—Regulated—Humane—You see these steers— healthful—watered—well fed—Into the slaughter pen they are driven—one by one—

Some women cry out at the smell—Some faint—Some turn back before they pass through the entrance—Some comment—how foul—Their fascinated disapproval—Some are sick—gagging when—Some scream when—stomach— intestines—shining—a gray color bruised—drop to the floor—

Nights you wake—your arms—body—performing a violent motion—a mallet into a steer's skull—How many times a night this enactment—Your dreams—Foremen shouting—din of slaughter—blood sluices—Chains clanging—pulley—conveyances—The skull is like a steel plate—the mallet—blood—a red mist—A door opens—the beast into the slaughterhouse slides—

You are not what you were—Your body—skin and hair—crevices—Your odor—blood stamped—meat—decay—shit—Stripped naked—before the basin—water heated—lavender perfumed soap—water discolored gray—blackening—yet still this musk—

What of this fragrance lies upon the skin—what from the body—emanates—Terror accelerates the blood—sours the meat—The—groans—bestial—alone surely infiltrate your flesh—transfigures—Shouts occasional—grunting—Doors opening—slamming—Blood spurting—flooding—Chains—wheels—machines—conveyer belts—groaning—rattling—Dull hacking—ripping—

Psychic cord—from hammer to arm to skull—yes—

A man face down in blood—His head turned—his face black with dirt—His eye—opened white—soulless—Another man—shot through the neck—shotgun spray—A man—fallen from a fire escape—a steak knife through his back—punctured lung—His neck broken in the fall—Around the body the cops mill—smoking cigarettes—laughing—*The stupid cocksucker*—The man's wife—dragged from the building—thrashing—cursing—spitting—Neighbors in bathrobes—undershirts—whisper—leer—

A man is chased across the street—a trio of men—the desperate—almost silent—struggle—The man kicked in the belly—ribs—face—They stomp at his head—his hands—arms covering—They kick him until he moves no more—then they resume kicking until he is unrecognizable—meat—bone—blood—They remove his wallet from his pocket—The gathered crowd says nothing—The fascination—only—

Trains—above ground—Hats—newspapers—Buildings on fire—

A man shot in the face—Splattered—the waitress—her face glistens with blood—She can't even scream—The assassin shot through the window—falls dead on the sidewalk—Her father—the restaurant owner—I don't give a shit who sent him—I'll string him up like a goddamn trout—

From—*the Illustrated History of*—

—bone ware—combs—imitation tortoise shell—The brain—a delicacy—the cheek meat—canned—the tongue—pickled—so fresh—or canned—the bones—broken up—transfigured into—foot oil—The hides—into leather—softened—upholstery—coats—The carcass—it is well known—is sent to the butcher—or to Europe by—cold storage—The shank bone—is New England bound—into—knife handles—The ankle and

knee—every particle of fat—and to Germany then—the refine-ment of sugar—Additionally—manufacturing fiber—electrical appliances—

Thompson finds you in the washroom—weeping—You've stripped to—shorts and undershirt—Your shorts pulled to your knees—Beside you—neatly folded—apron, trousers, shirt, shoes—In one hand—revolver to your temple—pressed—what familiar weight—And draped into your other palm—your cock—flaccid—*What the hell is this*—Thompson brays—

—elevated train—world passing—through windows—smeared—lights blur—stream—pipes dripping—steel beams—apartment buildings—concrete—brick—roof-tops—chicken coops—smoke—fire escapes—men and women—chatting—Faces reflected—blurring—A man falls to the floor—kicking and flailing and groaning—A woman begins screaming—hands over face—*Get him off of me*—she cries—Lights flickering—train shuddering and rattling—hurtling through the city—

You and Babe meet at a tavern—Here—on the radio—
the White Sox game—A man at the opposite end of the
bar—shouting—groaning—*Quiet you*—Babe says—A voice
describes the game action—*Shoeless Joe is up*—it says—*Here
comes*—*Cocky Collins now*—the unremarkable cadence—The
ball is flung—sometimes it is struck—sometimes men run—
sometimes they do not—the ghostly swell of the crowd at
the least action—

It isn't the game—Babe insists—so much as the device
conveying the game—His—fascination—the passage of
sound—through wire—the very atmosphere—*They've
attempted to tame what is beyond their authority*—he says—
normalize the weird—*Photographs*—*turn of the century*—*city
sky choked with wire*—*By 1911*—he says—*a man could stand in
New York City and speaking to his brother in Denver*—*Vacuum
tubes*—he says—*amplification*—*the blue glow*—*electrons*—At
home—he says—he turns the radio dial—advertisements—
popular music—preachers—news broadcasters—He settles
into the sounds between stations—The blurring of trans-
mission—static roars—ghostly remnants of speech—leans
closer to the device—as if listening to layers deeper—a tex-
ture unheard—In these places he hears what no other man
alive can—impossible noises—whispers—recitations—*The
dead*—he says—*in these places make their confession*—

He orders you each—a glass of beer—a shot of whiskey—You tell him about your thoughts—consumed by—death—killing—skulls—mold—shadows—faces—gasping—*I wake up—I can't breathe—I thrash around—My father*—Babe finally says—*thought the woods were filled with saboteurs—anarchists—He wouldn't walk into a room that hadn't first been inspected for assassins—Finally—he put a pistol in his mouth—and put a bullet through his brain—*

My father—you say—*taught me of affliction*—His body—limping—his eyes—swollen with pain—His ailment—what he called cancer—For years he allowed no doctor inside his house—Physicians would merely confirm what he intuited—My uncle—he said—was a glorious man— Then surgeons tore him open—dismembered him like a side of beef—A more terrible death you cannot imagine—I will not allow *butchers* to hack away at me—he said—I am a man—I will die like a man—

You tell Babe how you sat by your father's bed—the odors of disease and dying—You read aloud several poems—one about a spider—the ocean breeze—Only now did he doubt the death prognosis that had shadowed him your entire life—*Perhaps I will live a great many more years*—he said—*I have always been a terrible hypochondriac*—

I found him in a pool of his own blood—you tell Babe—

—the light of explosions along the horizon—hazed—smoke and fires—three thousand miles distant—and in dull afternoons the ocean breeze brings the dead—wire mutilated—sun cooked—They rise from the water—they clot the boardwalk—gulls pick at meat and bone—

Perhaps it is from this comes—the worm—invisible—

A man in top hat shouts into a bullhorn—*Liberty—Freedom—Death to tyrants*—A man coughs in a crowd—He is beaten—dragged off—

River banks—transients gathered—lounging—Bare faces—they eat from cans flame blackened—smoke cigars—

Newsboys shout through—surgical masks—The fotoplay—a man smiling stands before his air machine—Helmet and goggles—he waves—Chaplin—chased around a ship's deck by a jealous husband—a hatchet aloft—From the audience—a laughter muffled—

The long line of shops shuttered—desolate walk—Motorcars hurtle by—the seldom carriage—drivers masked—The bakery—barber—empty—None enter the pharmacy—but shout through the open door—a boy brings their purchases

Beneath the—elevated tracks—you and Babe lean against a concrete wall—condensation dripping—Babe smokes a cigarette—hurried drags—legs scurry up the stairs—faces—blank—dreary—oblivious—the vast mystery—Subway car jolting—How lean you are—Hunger makes you sleek—Your body moves easily—these others—fattened—slow—They mop their brows—The sickening tide of men—paunchy—soft—ruddy—gray—They eat sausages—from steaming carts—

There seems no limit to his conversation—Christopher Marlowe—Goethe—The Armenian Genocide—Socialism—Anarchism—Plato—Nietzsche—The name and manner of every bird he encounters—Soon you can no more follow his thought—he continues on his own—mixing—what he calls the common languages—French—Italian—Spanish—Latin—Greek—

Subtlest eyeliner—lipstick—now—foundation—contour—In the mirror now—*You see*—he says—*prettier than Gladys Cooper*—

He brings you to a clearing—the depths of the park—cattails and green water—peat swirling—Dragonflies—*Here*—he says—*we're alone—Nobody bothers coming out this far*—He hears—then sees—what he calls a beautiful specimen—He asks for the rifle—*Not that I don't trust your shot*—he says—*It's simply better this way*—Upon a branch—a bulb of gray and red feathers rests—Then it is gone—*See how perfect*—He holds out the mass—smear of blood—

Summer heat—unbearable air—You mop your brow with a handkerchief—stiff—yellowing—with old sweat—loosening with new sweat—You buy a paper from the newsstand—lie in the park—oak shade—From benches—hoboes—beg for change—You open the paper—read the headlines—What a vile world this is—A child's arm is found in the rubble of an explosion—the child herself is nowhere—A dog in the street—writhing and bucking—blood matted—groaning—slow agony into death—The city swells with blood—A man—mustache—wide ecstatic eyes—his mind blurred with hallucinogenics—murderer—rapist—perhaps—of his two sisters—Three little boys discovered—miles and days apart from each other—badly beaten and mutilated—hacked and sliced—a Swedish drifter—suspected of the crime—beaten— his face—unrecognizable—before the assembled press—A girl no more than twelve—her smiling photograph—what was her body in a tenement basement—moldering—

Babe takes you to a cafe—*You'll like this place*—he says—*very European*—He orders coffee—pastries—sits sipping from his little cup—with fork and knife he cuts into—flaking delicacy—berries—cream—*We aren't like the others*—he says—*You know that—don't you*—

The schoolteacher's door—is always open—There within he is—always mopping his brow—his neck—His upper lip— perspiration beaded—shadow of a beard no matter the hour—

His room—the pipe smoke—*I believe tobacco kills the worm*—he puffs—*or at least dulls its senses*—Later—His drunken eyes—he hands the bourbon bottle and a glass to you—another to Babe—

Perhaps the worm is already inside you—he says to Babe—pale—searching—dormant—

Mother—he says—*played beautifully—You can't imagine how she was—angelic—She floated into a room—Beethoven—Moonlight Sonata—Chopin—the Minute Waltz—Schubert—Impromptu No. 3 in G-flat Major—She had lovely hands—It tore my heart to watch them—Something so perfect—*

The great Victrola cabinet—there the black platter laid— From this is conjured—a sound—bombastic—terrifying—The schoolteacher is talking—his voice with reverence—flut- ters—as if he can scarcely hold on—*Beethoven—maestro—the greatest genius to walk this earth*—Then the squall pulls him under—His eyes squeeze shut—His hands—into fists— He beats at the arms of the chair—stabs at the air—in time—When the playing stops he opens his eyes—This swollen man—porcine—sickly—his breast heaving—His faint smile—when he remembers you are leaned in his doorway—He blots his throat and brow—handkerchief—stiff with sweat—*It doesn't bother you does it—the music—Perhaps the Fifth is too—furious—No we like to listen*—Babe tells him—*Good, good*—he nods—

Mother—he says—was correct—I have no feel for music—no talent, you understand—To love something more than your entire life—yet you are banned—Do you understand—

The worm—imperceptible—writhing—

From the schoolteacher's room—Caruso—*Vesti la Giubba*—The widow—lingers at his doorway—her eyes seem to glaze—hand pressed against her breast—now brushes away a tear—*What magic*—the schoolteacher sighs—*to have lived to this age—Vesti la Guibba*—Outside his room they gather—sounds of listening—breathing—coughing—shifting in place—Mill girls—the widow's daughter—When the disc crackles to a conclusion they applaud—Babe whistles—they cry out encore—Caruso—is beckoned from the darkness—revived—Caruso—eternal—miraculous—sublime—Caruso—dead at 48—peritonitis—Caruso—within a glass sarcophagus—displayed—

A man's voice captured and copied a million times over—made to play and replay into eternity—a man lies moldering and yet he speaks—It's monstrous—

The body by worm—infiltrated—transformed—made to devour itself—

So many thousand—shrouded—table clothes—blankets—bed sheets—Many are gathered as they are found—exposed— swelling—green—From death bed to—wagon bed to morgue hallway—heaped—Even men acquainted with decay—retch and gag—In this place—the forgotten dead—husks—green black—bloating—methane—carbon dioxide—hydrogen sulfide—the fluid of decomposition—purged from mouth and nose—The skin—sloughs—

I want to show you something—Babe tells you—*I want to show you something about yourself*—

He opens an album—his photographic art—A hundred—more—women alone—women upon men—men upon men—several men—women between them—gatherings of men and women—women in postures exotic—How impressed he is when—you show neither outrage nor—revulsion—only curiosity—*Who were they*—*were these acts posed*—*or acted fully*—He only smiles—*Here*—he says—*for you*—No more than a child—ringlets—before a mirror she poses—dimpled buttocks—Her eyes—You make no effort to hide your arousal—He is beside you now—his breath at your ear—his hand—opening your trousers—How your eyes close—you lean into his touch—*She's dead now*—he whispers—

He cannot convey—the sound of her voice—the sensation of her breath—The terrible limitation of a—fixed image—a replication—Yet you stare—*Tell me*—Babe insists—*what you would do to her*—Lips—you say—toes—armpits—buttocks—Every odor—pungent—foul—Every taste—

Babe leads you through streets of filth—bodies—vomit—trash—bottles—wrappers—tins—Men leaning against brick structures—leering—chattering—calling out—Men in furs—ragged—their hips—cocked—Wigs—beauty marks—faux

pearls—Men—painted—lipstick—eyeshadow—foundation—contour—Voices—perverse—silken—Youths—no
more than boys—lithe—nearly hairless—sublime—lead men
into corridors—caverns—places dimly lit—

She sits at the edge of the bed—legs crossed—nylons—at
the calf torn—the pale skin shows—She is talking about
her dreams—*Pictures*—she says—*a starlet*—In certain postures—lighting—the illusion is total—In others—this false
contour—this foundation—a darkening where new whiskers
poke through—This pose—a cigarette held—a wrist—limp—
the hand—flutters—wags—as she speaks—a gesture—meant
casually—You see it for what it is—an approximation—
practiced—refined—So too her voice—If you asked her she
would name them—her progenitors—She could place every
movement—phrase—from them derived—

I knew you'd be back—she says to Babe—Her smile—*Who's
your friend*—Her hand—red nails—moves against your
thigh—This approximation—this—idealization—an eleva-
tion—*We're going to devour you*—Babe told her—Her dreamy
starlet smile—*I know you are—darling—but please—I haven't
got all night*—

From—

COPS—AMBUSHED—from apartment windows—bullets—spray—*Photographs*—Cop bodies splayed—their hats—uniforms—shoes—tangled—Cop faces—grotesque—smeared blackly—

HIGH CLASS VAUDEVILLE—The Mola Electric Washer—a solution to the washday problem—Spiritualism—is it—Divine—Devilishness—Deception—WHAT SAYS THE SCRIPTURE—Have you had your milk quota today—Tender Sugar-Cured Canned Ham—a new taste Enjoyment for you—

A senator from Indiana—newspapermen—a member of the Health Department—dozens others—imprisoned for sedition—

Explosions—packages flung through windows—thrown from machines—Banks—Shops—The streets—

Your wretched bed—bulging springs—sheets soaked—stained—cum—

You tell him you aren't a homo—*Of course not*—he smiles—His—eyebrows—verging upon a single line—His lips on your neck—the gentlest suction—His hand massages your cock—You feel like you could explode—*Never when you were younger*—he asks you—*Not once did you admire your little friends*—*There was one time*—you said—your clothing removed—the blonde boy before you—his hard smooth body—wrestling on his bedroom floor—groaning and sweating and grinding against each other—cocks stiff—feverish—until finally—the two of you at once—While you tell the story—the sound of him masturbating—*Tell me about this boy*—he says—panting—*He was killed*—you say—*A house fire*—*They had to identify him by his teeth*—

Tar fumes—

In the moonlight—you can't remember what Babe looks like—Attractive—yes—a boy—yes—scarcely older than a child—So much of the world to him unknown yet—in this world—he moves about as king—Now his car—quieted and still—You look upon him—shadowed—You know he is watching you—He shifts—seat leather creaking—Between you—a silence—quickening—swelling—Finally—his voice—scarcely a voice—*I'm studying Sanskrit*—Now perhaps a cloud leaves the face of the moon for he sees you clearly—His eyes are wide—awed—*You're gorgeous*—he says—*You could be in pictures*—he sighs—*Better looking than Harold Lockwood*—His hand moves across your brow—to your chest—

Soon the city—banished—lights hazed—swelling—while before you—a swampland—long grasses—cattails— moon darkness—creatures—hooting—chirping—His car—parked—quieted—He is telling you about his bird watching—He comes here to observe them—You're nodding—You know nothing about birds—

He enjoys your room—he says—for the smells—the confinement—the staleness—the wallpaper peeling—the sounds of degradation—terror—screams—gunshots—vomiting— machines—sputtering—careening—colliding—He calls it the actual world—*This is what I've wanted my entire life*— he says—Your room—a bed—dresser—books—papers—a lamp—hotplate—through open windows—drunks—laughing—whispering—conspiring—vagrants shout—Christ to them whispers—glowers redly—From the blood the city was raised—returned to the blood—someday it will drown— Every idiot soul—gulping and thrashing and choking—A gray haze—commotion vigorous—trains—automobiles— bicycles—The sidewalk—chicken bones—broken glass—a man—blistered hands for a pillow—Sewer putrescence— Steam—Men—hats—suits—cigarettes—Women—office girls—skirts—blouses—clacking heels—

Christ—he says—*I just need to touch you*—By this he means— kiss—lick—suck—slap—puncture—bite—Many nights you awake—yet by sleep half-consumed—devouring each other—soon there seems nothing—a mass—struggling—

THE DEAD IN FRANCE—Add Pleasure to Duty—by taking your bath in a handsome sanitary tub—Fine plumbing adds value to a house—Everbest Nut Margarine is served on the tables of the—Best Families—MINSTRELS ARE COMING—a partial list of the performers—THOSE FRENCH MAIDS—Views of Women to Import Girls from Heroic France—

—terror various—ANARCHISTS—SOCIALISTS—INFLUENZA—THE KU KLUX KLAN—

A man running down the street—Police chase—beat him with night sticks—Screams—blood spray—a tooth—The crowd—gapping—murmuring—eventually wanders on—

—in all rooms other—apartment buildings—tenement structures—vast hives—The hallway lights flicker—burn out—the pool of moonlight at each end—In the darkness— scurrying rats—roaches—A pigeon—deranged—beats itself against the window—the walls—Door ajar—Police—milling—laughing—a woman shot through the belly—She crawled in her slip—a blood trail—Now shot through the back of the head—Her killer—the lover—turns the gun on himself—Shoots his face off—lying in the blood slop— burbling through his mess—Still alive—they'll bandage the dumb bastard up just so they can roast him alive—Another room—A trunk is delivered—FRAGILE—A woman opens this trunk using a key received—two weeks previous—She screams—she cannot stop—Within the trunk—a boy no more than seven years old—bound at his wrist—ankles— gagged—choked to death on his own vomit—The cops laughing—*Stupid fucking Pollacks—what did they expect—*

New letters now—*Cousin Dick*—she wrote—*Do you receives these—childish—missives of mine—Do you read them—No matter—I will imagine what I imagine—*

How   I   yearn—she   wrote—*My   heart*—she wrote—*wild—famished—*

—*weekends*—she wrote—*tennis—boys—she wrote— grinning—white toothed—insipid—athletic—great chests—Chet—she wrote—Andrew—David—Todd—hands— brute—searching—breath—tongues—bruising—*

This boy—Charles—perhaps—a blanket over darkened grass—the moon—uncovered—glowing—He pressed my shoulder—against the blanket—I struggled—spat—A little more—he whispered—kissing my neck—Mass of heat— muscle—his hands—my breasts—Now—his ear in my mouth—I bit until I tasted blood—He sounded like a kicked dog—What the fuck is wrong with you—

A man—she wrote—*driving gloves—goggles—his auto-mobile—a crawling pace—I thought—now he will pull alongside me—his window rolled down—Hop in—I'll give you a ride—Finally—I thought—I will stand on the edge of things—Now—I thought—anything can happen—*

—school assemblies—she wrote—*Government officials—balding men—white shirts—electricity—radio waves—peace—prosperity—The rush to the modern—Ladies—marry—bloom with children—tend to the hearth—ladies—the time is now to support our returning soldiers—Applause—handshakes—*

She wrote—*I won't marry*—She wrote—*I'll never bear children*—She wrote—*Life—a virus—contagion—*

These bastards—she wrote—*How did you fall for their— militaristic propaganda—Their utopia—when they just mean—killing everybody else—These bastards—she wrote—Modernity—she wrote—extermination—technology— vaporization—The skin—peeled back—she wrote—the rotten soul—festering—groaning—*

*This phony—dead world—they've invented—*she wrote—*I'll scream in their faces—show them something real—untempered— awful—Oh I know them—she wrote—those mannequins will just—swivel and gape—titter nervously—flush—grow* *indignant—If only I could tear open my—throat and chest—show them everything—*

—this broken jaw—she wrote—our—lost kingdoms—

How beautiful Babe is—stretching his figure so you may observe—how lovely—pale—slender—You almost weep to see him from certain angles—inviting you—from this position or that—*Ravish me*—his body says—*brutalize me—savage me*—You oblige with tenderness—Glorious flesh—closely you inspect—kiss—taste—every inch—even his pock scars—twisted and puckered strangely—

Babe—masculinity perfected—yet how easily you could bob his hair—make scarlet his lips—cupid's bow—gown him—slim and straight—sheathe his feet in heels—crown him with a headband spangled—

His voice—his eyes—when the sex compulsion overtakes him—Come here—he tells you— Sometimes a smile— faint—sometimes simply—a voice deepened—Smaller than you—he climbs atop you—grapples with you—seizes your throat—slaps your face—sharp wet crack—He calls you— *Dog—Beast—Oaf—Simpleton—Buffoon*—He commands you remove your shirt—trousers—shorts—He opens the windows and you stand nude—shivering—chattering— while he leans against the far wall—stroking his cock—his eyes—frenzied—*Fucking brute*—he says—bend over—

Babe—lust-crazed—insatiable—He fucks you upon the bed—lashes you with a belt—smears you around the sheets—fucks you against the wall—your face beat into the plaster—fucks you upon the floor—your knees—aching—against floor boards—your ass—high in the air—His prick slathered—pungent—fluid discolored—As small as he is he will rip you in two—Babe laughs from the bed while you stagger about like an elderly man—your chest—hips—shoulders—back—ass—discolored yellow—green—purple—

What brought him into your life—fortune inconceivable—His proclivities are your own—Many occasions Babe speaks and you believe it your own voice improved upon—Perfected—Formulations of language you would never consider now uttered with ease—He says the same of you—*I saw Richard*—he will someday tell the press—*and somehow I knew—things he could confess before no other—we held in common—*

How you fear this dream's rupture—In bed beside you—gorgeous assemblage of eye—teeth—fingers—cock—navel—fine soft hair—lips—full—red—his breath—the breath of life—his fluid—from whence life emerges—

—warm rapture of—his skin against your skin—

Newspaper stands—magazines—Crowding men—Coins—Men buying cigars—morning papers—Cigar smoke—Headlines—Murderers—Executions—Saboteurs—Bombings—Bodies—like discarded animals—on the sidewalks—fire escapes—library steps—

A girl—gone into nothingness—Her photograph—finally—upon the front page of the morning papers—*How sad*—a woman said—*What a homely girl*—said another—

Her favorite outfit—blue sailor frock—blue oxfords—She wore no stockings—

This girl and her friends—stopped at a shop window to admire—magazine covers—McCalls—Summer Fashion Number—a woman—showered with cherry blossoms—Motion Picture—Lillian Gish in a bonnet—*the Saturday Evening Post*—barbed wire—German shepherd in Red Cross garb—*Vogue*—a woman bejeweled astride a swan—

Neighbors—local children—shopkeepers—search the parks—sidewalks—shops—They call out her name—There is a reward—Many telephone in—having seen her—sucking ice chips—loitering train stations—

The police search—brutal—meticulous—alleyways— beneath garbage piles—basements—coal bins—They dredge the lake—find cow bones—chicken joints—Haul in every moron—halfwit— submental—they can find—*Look at these brutes—fucking disgusting*—the chief tells the assembled press—

I've been thinking about you—she wrote—

How young we were—at grandmother's—You were—no more than—fifteen—When you walked to the pond—pole and tin bucket—how I trailed after you—How you ignored me—skipping along—whistling—singing—calling out to butterflies—grasshoppers—I close my eyes—and the pond glares—with morning light—No time has passed when I close my eyes—You still sit smoking upon a rock—dried weed—the cool humid air—In the mud—boney remnants of fish—Run along now—you tell me—What pleasure it gives me—to pretend to ignore you—to risk your ire—I remove my shoes—step to the mud—little feet in the gray muck—You smile—Your smile broke my heart—Oh Dickie—you were the most beautiful boy in the world—I'll never forget how you said—You're a goddamn pest you know—How you cast your line—while I stood watching—

There—is an old woman—on a park bench—brushing her face—slapping—*Can nobody help me*—she murmurs—Now she screams—*Ants—ants—please help me*—Babe is laughing—Later you say to him—*Somebody should take care of that old woman—it's disgusting*—Babe regards you—*What would you do*—he finally asks—*Hit her with a brick—throw her in the fucking river—I don't know*—

An execution—the papers are obsessed with it—He shot a priest—two cops—They found him hiding under a car—shot through the arm—passed out in a pool of blood—Three years later they strapped him into a mechanism—leather and wire and wood—He refused his final meal—To his family he left a letter—*The hour of departure*—he wrote—*has arrived—What I'd do to see that*—you said—Babe looks up from your cock—shining with his slobber—*What do you think it smells like*—he says—

When now you hear Beethoven—Brahms—from the teacher's apartment—Babe groans—*I'd like to string that fat fuck up—Open his neck—drain him clean*—

*I dreamed you died—*she wrote*—I know you'll understand how terrible this felt—You were laid out on a table—They pulled back the sheet—He was killed instantly—someone said—From the neck up—you seemed to be asleep—Your mother was there—My darling—beautiful boy—She said to me—I clipped a lock of his hair—Here—she says—You can have some—*

*There are no more cemeteries—*she wrote*—no more burials— Now we house in the dead in towers of glass—We can look upon them whenever we wish—We are never separated—not really—*

I saw you—your hands and lips to the glass—pressed—

You had no more color—except—the stitching—black— red—enflamed—from your groin—to throat—They cut you open—removed every organ—replaced your blood with—preservative—made you impervious to time—

You were speaking—but through glass—every word—muffled—lost—

Evenings now—You and Babe patrol the streets in his car—What young giggling figures you see—pony tails—skirts—*You like that one—don't you*—says Babe—They are not to his taste—Yet—he enjoys how you leer—

You and Babe—your elbows on the counter—The soda jerk brings you a cherry Coca-Cola—Babe—a malted milk—

Her friends—at a table—strawberry—chocolate—marshmallow—ice cream sundaes—Little spoons—lips dappled white—They are laughing—If she sees you—she does not notice your attention—Her friends—the tall one—slender—pink lips—the other—shorter—fuller—her complexion—ruddy—curled hair—This one catches you—she glances away—whispers to her friends—

In Babe's car you follow them—at a distance—The group—splinters off—you follow her—Across the street—you park—sit—smoking—Her father's house—*The old bastard*—you say—Babe laughs—*These are lesser people*—he says—*You want her—she's yours—Anything in the world—Any sweet little girl—it's yours—I promise—There's nothing they can do against you*—

How easily—you thought—I can enter—Break down the window—Kick through—the front door—I push past the Pollack girl—absurd in—French maid's attire—Slap the mother down—She's sprawled—weeping—screaming—The old man—confused—*What the hell are you*—He outweighs me—but he's fat—soft—A quick swat to the windpipe and—he's wheezing from his knees—She is in her bedroom—her little desk—textbook and pencil before her—Her bare neck—shoulders—

There are more letters—They pile upon your desk—This other you—this—not you—Somewhere he stood—perhaps—this city—You close your eyes—imagine—his outline—You saw him—a shadow—entering a room of—furious light—

Petty atrocities Babe helps you commit—out of what he calls—amusement—sport—A brick thrown through a window—an alarm is triggered—the two of you flee— watch from behind a tree—darkened side street—The police arrive—*You'll love this*—Babe whispers—He strolls out— Chatting with the cops—pointing—The officers show their lights in that direction—Soon the shop owner arrives— Babe stands gesturing—describing—elaborating—Finally he returns to you—broad grin—*You see how easy it is—I could've thrown the brick in front of them in broad daylight and they would've believed me when I said two Hungarians did it—*

How easily—he says—*to get a drop on a couple of them—I have no animosity toward the police*—Babe says—*Human nature insists the powerful must tend toward corruption—greed—It is the natural order—for the most vile to assume such positions— You see it in most every species—The difference—he insists—is in nature there is no moral judgement—no handwringing—There is simply struggle—murder—survival—*

*We stand on the outside of them—he says—No where else in nature does what we are exist—They have no authority over us—*You nod—You have felt this your entire life—

The plan begins—a prank—The capture—debasement— of a policeman—stripped naked—perhaps—suspended from a lamp by his ankles—gagged—moaning—By early morning he will have—twisted and thrashed himself insensible—red—purple—*What a sight*—Babe slaps his thigh—

Masks are purchased—Rope—Babe you teaches you a knot—unbreakable—*The more the swine struggles*—he says—

Every cop you pass now—the two of you—snickering—whispering—*He better watch himself*—

Babe knows about chloroform—the rag soaked—inhaled— how the pig will drop—A trial run—first—a street otherwise deserted—lamplights—evening haze—open windows—a victrola—Caruso—Gounod's Faust—couples shouting—If someone should glance out the window—No—it is better this way—You stop the first man who passes—ask—the time of day—Two men chatting stroll past—the opposite side of the street—*The time is given*—Babe says—*Let's go—We've been seen—*

You lose interest in cops—*What is a cop—but power—authority—made a cudgel—The mayor—his cronies—a senator—a millionaire—his house—ransacked—his family—tarred—feathered—his children—raped—his wife*—Babe stops you—

Not atrocity for the sake of atrocity—he fondles your cock—his eyes—what delight—*Atrocity*—he says—*perversion—because it pleases us—We will rape the wife only if she appeals to us—you say*—Babe laughs—*Precisely—*

We will capture an orphan—a wild street child—a lean pretty little boy—sooty little face—His jacket—frayed and filthy—We'll lead him to—your father's house—you say—My father is dead—Babe answers—*Your grandmother's house*—Babe nods—*We'll feed him—steak—potatoes—milk—We'll fatten the little thing up—*

*We'll—feed him whiskey—tie him to the bed—lash him—
throw acid in his face—sodomize him—When he is used
up—we'll leave him in the street—naked—blind—
gagged—hogtied—castrated—Bleed him out—a dying little
piggy—*

*We will need a house—you say—with at least a dozen rooms—
One room for every child we acquire—*Babe smiles—*Of course
darling—*

She wrote—*There was a room—There were others—We were all dressed in black—black veils—glasses—We stood before—phonographs—discs labeled with—the names of our dead—whirling—A silence—crackling—then—your name—After all these years—I heard again your voice— clear and immediate—as if announcing answers upon command—First—your name—then a recitation—steady— the Appomatox—Gallnipper—the Three Brothers—George W. Morely—Grace Channon—SS Chicora—There were many others—But you know this—*

Interlude II: 1974

Here are all versions—

The president—disgraced—before a desk—papers—his speech— His words—the sounds of a man—condemned—There is no longer the need—he says—for the process to be prolonged—His gray face—sickly with sweat—shadow of stubble—I would have preferred to carry through to the finish—whatever the personal agony—the interest of the Nation—must always come before any—personal considerations—His eyes become glossy—far off—he shuffles through the pages—he has lost his place—perhaps some aide—put the pages in the incorrect order—the Soviet Union—he mutters—the Middle East—1000 million Arabs— he says—then he is quiet—searching—finally—Checkers—he says—The old man has been in the sherry again—reporters whisper—The president continues—nodding now—He has found his stride—Arab countries—Latin America—Africa— Asia—the People's Republic—China—He continues—a Congressman—a Senator—a Vice President—a President— The words flow easily now—World peace—he says—Nuclear arms—he says—I have long taken heart—he says—from a poem by T.S. Eliot—The eyes are not here—the president recites— this valley—dying stars—hollow valley—broken jaw—We grope— together—avoid speech—on this beach of the—tumid river—Sightless—unless—eyes reappear—star perpetual—mul- tifoliate—rose—death's—twilight kingdom—The hope only—of empty men—

Shadow worlds—truths—

You sons of bitches have ruined me—the president says—his swollen eyes—upon the press—

Slowly—gravely—he calls out the names of cabinet members— Where's Henry—he says—come up here Henry—The president hands over a manilla envelope—Just hold onto that for now— there are some things in there for you—Other officials—one by one—they too are given envelopes—There's something in there for Harriet as well—Now—from a final envelope—calmly he removes a magnum revolver—At last—within the crucial moment—he is at ease—

There are cries—the secret service begin to move—The president waves them all back—

Stay back—he says—Leave the room if this will affect you—Don't—don't—he says—this will hurt someone—

Slow the video now—he clasps the revolver in two hands—one hand upon the long barrel—the other—the handle—trig- ger—His mouth—widening—impossible chasm—so too his eyes—exhilaration—terror—the muzzle—directed into his mouth—a pop—
He is standing—he drops—blood geysers—his mouth and nose—the top of his head—He's shot—a woman screams—Oh shit—a man's voice—Dick stop—Dick—Oh shit—the same

man—says more loudly now—Settle down—don't panic—Settle down—a man's voice over the others—dull—flat—Someone call—Someone call the ambulance—

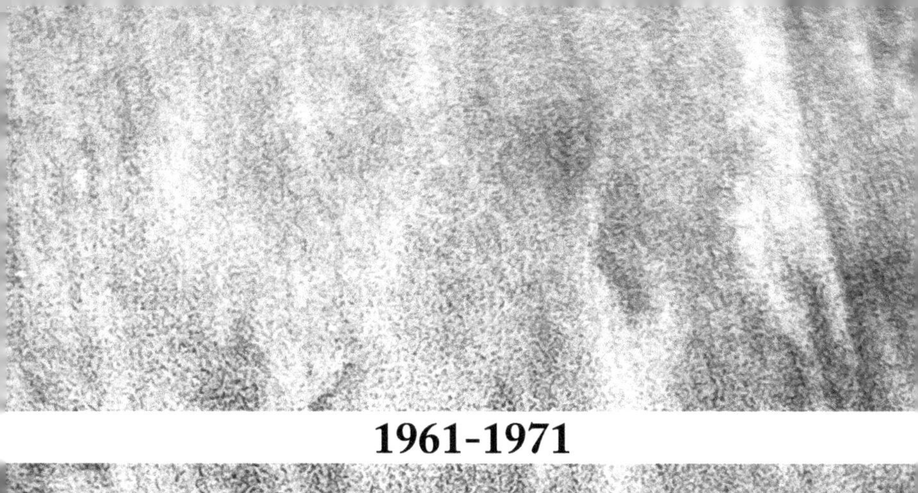

1961-1971

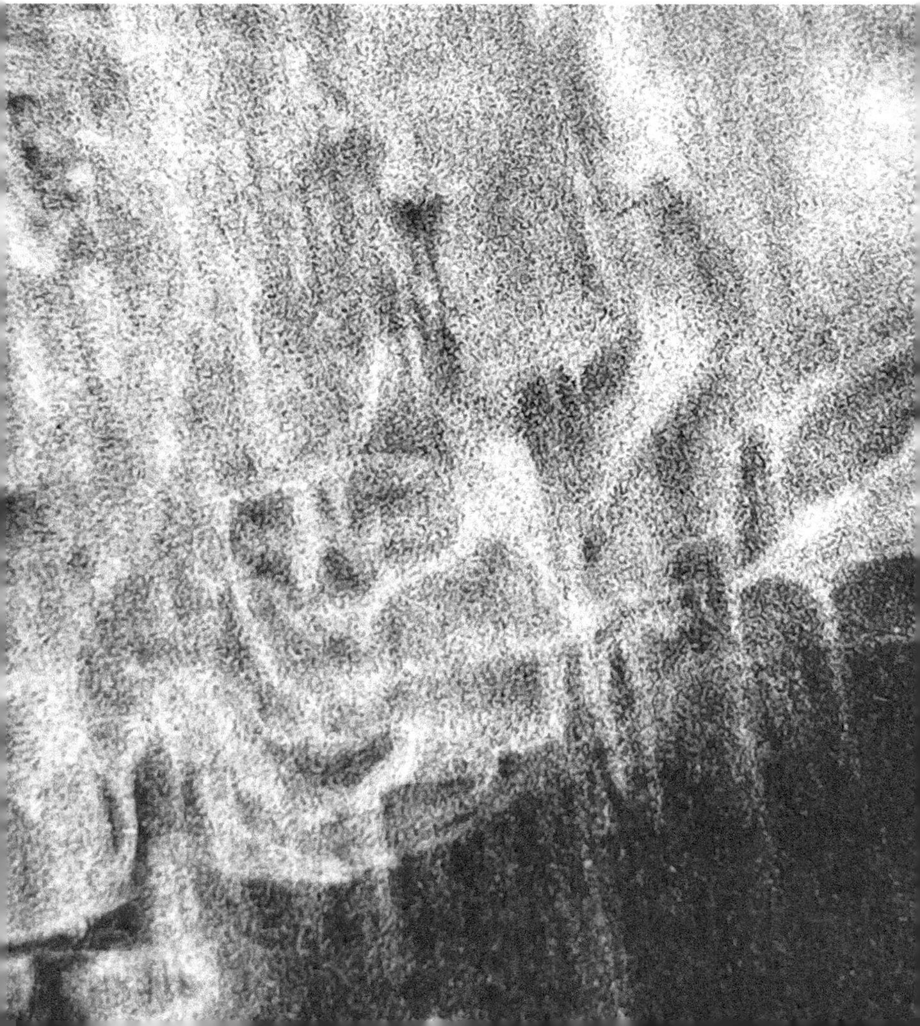

He died a most terrible death—Clara says—I was privy to it all—What a wonder is a man—transformed—slowly—

The televisions—these screens I cannot escape—room after room—declare it nearly before I know it myself—

Quiet these—I tell the girl—*He is dead now—we do not need this—constant sound—*

Slowly the din dissolves—the mute mouths continue—Images—still—moving—They depict a young man—Top hat—white scarf—Brows—thick—black—Before a black board—marks of chalk—Equations—Theorems—incomprehensible—He is smiling even—

Is this the man I knew—Is this the man he was—

They show him with his wives—his many wives—his children—How many children—Perhaps they are saying their names—these lives—no more than flies—No—he was not a man—he was closer to a god—a sheet of sun—

He would tell you a story—He would say—*I discovered her*—one amidst a thousand women—He would tell you—

I handled his private affairs—yes—His correspondence—his meetings—I arranged his travel—see him dressed—fed—

I have blotted the fever from his brow—allowed him lean on me when too weak for a cane—I have found him collapsed—trembling—ignorant of his surroundings—my name—

He discovered me—Clara says—a young woman—seated before a typing machine—He was the greatest man this world has ever known—

Sometimes I thought—My childhood—mother—father—St. Louis itself—My every memory—a phantasm—he whispered into my ear—

Sometimes I thought—When he closes his eyes—When his mind expires—Do I persist or wink out—figment of his soul—

The papers call him—notorious—No—he had his fascinations is all—

The funeral—the great church—arrangements of flowers—He lies in state—His wives and children—associates—senators—

They assume—perhaps—I was his lover—

We all owe him a tremendous debt—they tell me—*His tragedy was not his device but—his renunciation of his device—*

The screens depict—Athleticism—Men armored—hurtling against each other—mud and grass—They lie—piled—They pry themselves apart—One man writhes upon his back— Another—spits blood—Faces watching on—exhaling clouds—A frenzy of images now—The name of a deodorant flashes across the screen—A man upon a horse—lassoing a calf—the calf falls and the man drags it across the dirt—The name of a toothpaste—an animated ghost smiling—cavorting—A woman in a blue gown—blonde—stands behind a seated man—cross legged—a dinner jacket—red velvet—a white scarf—He is smoking a cigarette—in his other hand—a glass of bourbon—He is exhaling smoke—speaking now—a sip of his drink—speaking again—The name of an automobile flashes across the screen—The screen depicts—a man clutches a rope—pulls it taut across a beautiful woman's alabaster throat—Her red lips—seem to smile—Pulls it through her throat—her expression—contorts—*I should like to hear this one*—I tell the girl—The sound is returned—The

room fills with—seconds—luxuriant—gagging—wheezing—heavy breathing—How wide her eyes—How flushed
he is—What a display—How relentless this man is—No
one in his life suspects him capable—Then the dull thud—
the woman's legs—black stockings—a shoe cast off—the
man on hands and knees—gasping—*Enough*—I tell the
girl—*It is over*—

Upon the screens—the trial—This man shows no shame—I thought—*They will hang him and it is right*—Robert said—*They should do the same to me*—

What is it to admire a man who repudiates himself—You could cleave the world in two—I did not tell him—Your device—

To hold the scythe aloft—The second city—what they must have felt—awaiting their fate—

Have I been alive this entire time—

There is nothing not shown on these screens—from room to room I may walk—A great wilderness—three thousand miles away—A little girl—naked—runs screaming—burning—a man is executed—the blood from his head—sprays— Orange flashes over the forest vastness—Then there is dancing—singing—laughter—unearthly—unseen faces— as if from afar—Men playing guitars—a beautiful slender woman—her portly friend—voices angelic—Two men in— costume resplendent—The younger—an orphan boy taken in—Together they live in the older man's mansion—They cavort about in—capes—masks—They solve crimes—One suspects they are—lovers—

There are delicious words—murder—torture—rape—

Others—atrocity—genocide—rich and evocative—
one reclines mouthing them—a glass of bordeaux—a
cigarette—One's head—swims—

Bodies skeletal—from ditches—heaps—Bodies in pris-
oner's clothing along fences—standing—hands through
chain link—rungs—*How did this happen*—a man behind
a desk says—

They commemorate Robert's device—a cloud—
momentous—light and wind—trees and
houses—swept away—The world before Robert—and
the world—after—Robert's vast legacy—Hairless—fea-
tureless—sculptures of ash—char—yet—staggering—A
child—pries herself from a building collapsed—Skin like
a glove—from her arm pulled—She does not scream—A
man—fights against his rescuers—runs into—a city
burning—His—fruitless—anonymous—immolation—

This woman—her very particles—warped—Her brain—her
throat—stomach—with disease—inflated—They will carve
her open—remove the affliction—On a plate—wrapped
in blood—it will glow—The affliction will return—and
return—and return—*I was murdered twenty years ago*—she

says—*yet still I walk the earth*—*Hibakusha*—she says—*have the blood of the devil*—

I would like to meet her—I say—*Can we not arrange such a meeting*—

The Bright New Look—Years and years of dependable service—Formica—Cherries within—pineapple spirals—caramelized—cakes sodden in juice—sugar—bourbon—A woman—weeps—her hands inflamed from—washing dishes—Her husband no more goes to her at night—So automatic it—lowers the bread itself—Soup for lunch—in only six minutes—the children—smile and smile—and mother is so relaxed—This animated doll—walks—spins—her head—flirts—she wails—The cleanest—sheets in town—From—suds to spin dry—a housewife ecstatic—gone now those—traumatic hours—Exciting—mealtime magic—a young man hands his father—a frozen—steak—Linoleum—How the floors—shine—Shrimp—cocktail—they suck the sauce—clean off—The husband spanks his—naughty wife—she squeals—A salad—bright green—gelatinous—carrots—celery—ham—suspended—quivering—Steel kitchens—shine—the woman clasps her hands over her breast—her smile—radiant—Chrome—Finally—a real freezer—A bee holds a spoon—desirous of ice cream—The end of after meal clutter—

A marvelous device—really—all manner of delicacy—preserved—Pink marbled flesh of—beef—Catsup—chocolate cake—side of—ham—Peas—milk—Coca-Cola—red marbled flesh of—watermelon—purple grapes on a dish—clustered—Leaf lettuce—How long one can hold their arm against—frozen steaks—particles of ice—before one's arm—blues and numbs—How long before the pain—delicious—sublime—becomes unbearable—O now we will see—I can last forever—

I wanted to annihilate myself—Robert said—

Within this—vessel—this—so-called—jetliner—quaking—rocking—hurtling through the atmosphere—one senses more immediately the—nearness—of annihilation—The veil here made obvious—the adornment of activity—beauty—chatter—Feasts brought forth on—carts—silver trays—Baked ham—orange and—clove sauce—Cornish hens—Glazed—yams—Peas aux Beaurre—Salade d'Asperges—Pencil skirts—long legs shapely—Would you desire anything further ma'am—the girl leans closer to me—eyeshadow—silver—her red scarf—her orange—pillbox hat—Her—pink—waiting—lips—They drink themselves foolish—Scotch—Mai Tais—Martinis—Gimlets—Manhattans—Cigarette smoke bluely coiling—noxious haze—Men—married yet—without constraint—a hand strokes a stranger's bare knee across the aisle—obscenities whispered as they are served—Within this place the old rules are meaningless—

The papers will say—the great man's secretary longs to meet his—million children—*What should you like to see*—my guide asks—How I long to see what it was—I do not say—the rubble and lines of trees—burned clean—The children—incubated in wombs—transfigured—I do not say—I would taste—what holy ash and bone—I would—lie down in ruin—seething—

My guide—The dome—copper melted—left a husk—Every-one within killed—See here it yet stands—a monument to—universal peace—the guide says somehow without laughing—What remarkable restraint these people have—*The bomb*—the guide gestures to the sky—her voice—reverent—pleasant—She sees nothing of what she describes—*Shima Hospital—a wave of heat—3,000-4,000 degrees—Winds—roared—through the entire city—Flames consumed—every building—incineration—rubble—ashes—Were you here*—I interrupt—*Oh no*—she smiles—She was just a little girl then—raised in some distant city—*One heard the news reports—a mysterious weapon—a city disappeared in—light—*

I use the words she expects to hear—*Oh yes—How terrible—How awful*—She expects me to weep—I am practiced at such performances yet—my tears have always felt—unconvincing—

It is a—splendid city—I tell my guide—*One senses everywhere the residue of Robert's device—They can build and rebuild—yet—they will never remove it—*

Finally I am brought to—the woman—Through—sliding doors of paper and wood—a room furnished in the—Western style—Beside me on the sofa—my guide—across from us—the woman smiles politely—We are—served a—fragrant tea—I am shown a—photograph of her as a child—She is smiling—her mother and younger sister—her father briefly home from the war—One year before the bomb—she is a child as any other—

Her practiced speech—*I looked down at the city—there was nothing—We couldn't understand what happened—Within hours—the lights were returned to us—Within days we had—running water—The spirit of the people was—amazing—*

Yes—I say—*but what did it sound like*—She blinks—*Sound*—she says slowly—*Your mother—your sister—did you see them*—Quietly—soothingly—I say—*I want you to describe them*—I touch the bare skin of—her arm—The guide looks down—now slowly she translates—The woman's eyes fill with a shimmer not seen before—She pulls away from my hand—I lean forward—*When did you sense you were no more yourself*—She is confused—The guide tries again—*When did you realize you were—transformed—*

She tells me about her headaches—lethargy—the doctors—It is no use—Robert's device was wasted on this woman—

I would have them enshrined—frozen in their—most perfect state—flesh and organ and blood—blooming with—impossible light—Monument of glass—one could walk along for hours—stopping when one likes—Bodies—crumpled—blackened—one longs to pull the once-skin

in strips—Bodies no more than—shadows on concrete—
Bodies with—affliction—brimming—Bodies—their
eyes—dissolving—bleeding—Bodies of half ash—A
sudden gust would—This one I command speak—and
now—a jaw—teeth—moves—a voice distant—echoing—
unmoored—from flesh—human will—mediocrity—*I was a
man once—I remember nothing of that time—plodding—eating—
shitting—Then a flash—Then this—nothingness—Now I fill a
void—No contour or shape—Now—nothing—everything—*

I would turn to Robert—Robert—his porkpie hat—his
pipe—His eyes radiating—light—*Now—I would say—you
understand—what a beautiful thing you've done—*

I should like to see Robert again—I tell the maid—

In Robert's screening room—the device whirs—Robert
on the screen—cast in light—gray and black—His mouth
moves—there is no sound—Robert—as I never knew him—
How frail he seems here—Robert as he ever was—desolate
in his guilt—*He understood nothing*—I say—

Robert wooed me—a single red rose each day—delivered to
my door—A gift—anonymous—yet only Robert could—

I saw you—he said—*A man knows*—*the will submits to some force*—*higher*—

Robert's vehicle—a horrendous mechanism—glass and steel—fins—leather—His tan kid gloves—The radio station—flickers—Glenn Gould—*the Goldberg Variations*—This man—what frenzy—his fingers—In the darkness—the road beneath us—flees—The country—wild—around us—the forest alive—Faster—I want to say—Head-lamps-a low illume—the road—bends and curves—sudden turns—We are hurtling at a speed—obscene—yet I long for—acceleration—

What he calls—a house—atop a hill—the win-dows—dozens—lighted—in the darkness total shines a structure—as if burning—The gates are open—the long drive—gravel—bones under tires—breaking—

His ancient house—furnished in modern style—He tells me of—former occupants—General Washington—he says—The paintings hanging upon the walls—A sunflower—A man—pale—inconsolable—A woman—blue—corpselike—arms folded across her lap—He tells me their names—authors—

Robert prepares—steaks and asparagus—My mouth full of—blood—butter—He pours me a martini—My head swims—

Back and forth before the hearth—burning—Robert

paces—*Speak to me in Greek*—Robert says—*I will answer you in Latin*—*I don't know Greek*—I say—*Nec refert*—he replies—

He recites—*a youngling bird*—*in its nest*—*trembling*—*I'll pluck his heart right out*—*within its own blood*—*drowned*—Robert finishes—smiling—sips his martini—

Robert fills my glass—again—*Nobody goes thirsty in this house*—he insists—

Robert sits next to me—*I know nothing of physics*—I tell him—*mathematics to me is a mystery*—*gibberish*—He waves abruptly—*I don't care*—he tells me—*Darling*—*I'm enraptured with you*—

His voice—tender—jocular—*To the pretty girls I say*—*I want to look like you*—*To the pretty girls I say*—*I want you to look like me*—

There are many rooms within this house—Robert tells me—*Floors I alone may access*—

Within one room—white walls—the floor—Night stand—
lamp shades—orange—A bed—covered white—There laid
out—accoutrement—lacy—black—

Now I will learn—what a man such as Robert—

I wore here my best dress—Yet now it lies—a
red skin—satin—bodiless—across the bed—
Yet now I stand—shivering—stockings, garter,
suspenders—panties—sheer—brassiere—Heels—spiked—

Yet I—stand shivering—A room—hearthless—This room
alone perhaps in all this great house —without heat—

My arms—hands—over—skin rising—My breath—a
whiteness—A room of white walls and floor boards—A
room—windowless—A room—unseen—unknown—A
rug—gold and red and green—every thread and strand—by
hand—woven—Perhaps—a dozen girls—their blood and
perspiration—Perhaps in this room—Washington's servants—and whoever to them crept at night—Perhaps—the
whiteness of the walls—Every footfall—every booted foot—
every stocking—Upon the bed—every cry of passion—Am
I the first to so stand here attired—

Then the lights are deadened—Lamp shades—a paper skin—dim—then—a darkness—absolute—

A voice—in the room—yet not in the room—a voice Robert's yet—hollow—echoing—*Turn*—it says—*your back to the door*—When slowly I turn—When I face the windowless wall—*Your eyes*—it says—*must be shut*—When I leave them open—the frailest—peep—it says—*Strain them shut*—

Now I will—what Robert—

Amid vast ocean spaces—far from human habitation—a remote chain of—coral islands—In less than a minute—the most powerful explosion—witnessed by human eyes—The Thermonuclear Era—Quickly their eyes—goggled black—A madman's brain—gray—shifting with fire—disease—swelling—An island entire—removed from existence—islands nearby—stripped of life—One hundred miles distant—children play in ash—Their skin—blistering—molting—Any capital city—New York—London—Paris—Annihilation—total—The universe swallowed by flame—wind—Flutes—oboes—great patriotic moans—An orchestra—rises—

I have watched the ocean waters—lashed by light—frenzied—heat and motion—Fish—boiled alive—clot the beaches—eyes whitened—The face of the earth remade—crimson and black—

Did not some force similar vanquish beasts—primordial—Perhaps such a man as Robert existed then—Perhaps we have all been bathed in his light many times over—We would remember nothing—

Yet—there are certain deeps—by Robert—untouched—There creatures move ignorant—

What fatal hour—beyond return—we cannot know or see—
Robert said—We are led across the terrible line—unbeknownst
to us—The atmosphere quivers with—genocide—unrealized—

Two streams of experience—One—we stand within—Here
we have known—the sin of annihilation—Within the world
other—we languish—the greater sin of—ambition—throttled—

In 100 years—this planet extinguished—a dead rock—
blackened—Yet we will have known—the desert swollen
with—light—

On the screens—

Children—portrayed as apes—ghoulish eyes—wire tails—
One pretty monkey—pert little breasts—A simian caravan
now—they ride their bicycles to a picnic lunch—Through
negligence—one after another—maimed—slaughtered—by
vehicles careening—quiet streets—They are not depicted in
their oblivion—yet one imagines clearly—broken necks—
furry limbs—mangled—*How foolish*—a voice—clucks—*Just
this once—they broke the rules*—Finally—the careful child—
arrives at the park—Greedy monkey before his hoard of
paper sacks—*Only one—becomes fat*—the voice says—

Sirens—children cower beneath school desks—a man
dives behind his sofa—A white flash—a woman within
her raincoat—crouches—

Homosexuals—prowling—pencil line mustaches—black
eyes—A voice warns—*Boys—beware—perverts come—cloaked
as sheep*—One such homosexual—his merry prance affected
masculine—his effeminate lisp—deepened—befriends a
boy—Together they fish by the brook—*Call me Charles*—
whispers the homosexual—*Mr. Johnson is my father*—The boy
laughs—Now the homosexual suggests a friendly smoke—
Your father will never know—The veneer begins to fray—a
voice intones—From his jacket the homosexual retrieves a—
gold cigarette case—the cigarettes—Turkish—The boy hacks

and gags and the homosexual smiles—his legs crossed in the—feminine manner—purple socks—*Young Davey*—the voice says—*should know better*—*the signs are all there*—Yet when the homosexual shows the boy—certain Polaroid photographs—he does not look away—He flushes—One senses his excitement—*Gee whiz Charles*—whispers the boy—*these are something*—*Davey does not know*—says the voice—*his fatal path is set*—The child is led up the motel steps—Sadly the camera does not follow—yet the mind knows—

A flash of light—how quickly the house untended—burns— The neighboring house—freshly painted—white—the leaves raked—the clutter cleaned—unscathed—

A girl—unkempt—haphazard in her motivation—needlework unfinished—her outfit not prepared the previous night—her hair unbrushed—her shirt—blotched—She must hide the stain with a sweater—The other girls discuss—a popular novel—she nods and feigns—knowledge—*Oh yes*—she says—*quite thrilling*—*Barbara*—a voice chides—*How foolish you are*—*How slovenly*—*Barbara*—*Barbara*—*Barbara*—*Do you want to die alone*—The other girl—methodical—Her perfect—hair, complexion, figure—*You see Susan*—says the voice—*Vivacious*—*poised*—*interesting*—*Susan practices the piano*—*Susan does not go parking with boys*—*Susan is beloved*—*Barbara*—*She is everything you are not*—

I should like to hire a maid—Robert tells me—

They come wearing—great heavy coats—fur collars—snow heavy—Soon they stand in the front room—dripping—I sit in my chair—I apologize—There is no one to take their attire—They shift—coats in arms—*You see why we so desperately require help*—I say—

I say—*Tell me about yourself*—Soon enough I know—who is unsuitable—So many are—too assured—competent—How they long to clean every speck from this room—They have no appreciation for filth—clutter—I seem to listen—as they list for me their experience—*Yes, yes*—I say—*Impressive, really*—

Then there are those—desperate girls—Uncertain—fidget-ing—Their coats too thin for the cold—They shiver—feign warmth—comfort—confidence—

This one darkly complected—her downward glances—She is but—sixteen—seventeen—though she insists nine-teen—No doubt she lives now in a hovel—a wretched place—Some man has—within her—manufactured within a child—One can tell with these girls—She left it to the nuns—perhaps—One prefers to think—she had it mur-dered—Some—general practitioner—spread her open—the affliction—removed—discarded—

Was he an older fellow—I do not ask—Your father's dear friend—Did he ply you with drink—sweets—whisper endearments—Perhaps you believed he would—whisk you from the dreariness—Perhaps you enjoyed it—even pleaded for it—Yes I see your sly glances—your little grins—I see how your tongue does traipse along your teeth—You are a foul one—

We costume her in the austere manner of her office—black and white—skirt and stockings—One admires the whisper of leg—calf and knee—She strains for the high corners—feather duster—toe tips—

One wants to command her—*Remove your shoes—dear—* One longs to—see there the sweet little toes—webbed in black—One wants to run their fingers along—lovely arch of foot—One longs to—moisten stocking—with breath—tongue—to nibble—

Robert—smoking his pipe—his finger along a bookshelf—there the filth—He smiles—*She is the worst maid I have ever seen—*

We invite our maid to dinner—Darling girl—she wears a—
cotton dress—navy—polka dots—imitation pearls—Robert
would feed her steak—but I insist upon Cornish hens—crisp
little corpses—How carefully we dismember them—forks
and knives—bone and tender flesh—ligament and skin—
vein—Lovely little bodies we—suck from bone—savor and
chew—Robert would have her imbibe martinis—I insist
on Bordeaux—Fine delicate lips—glazed red—Hold still
dear—I say—lean closer so—with a napkin now I slowly
dab—My body—a pressure against her—Robert smiles—

This first maid we re-attire in our savage way—pale
skin—Surprising voluptuousness of the breasts—buttocks—
Lace—fabrics sheer—Slowly I pull shoes onto—wiggling
feet—We bind her wrists—behind her back—Her ankles—
Frail wooden chair—creaks and groans—A rag fills her
mouth—Her eyes—slowly comes a clarity—

We stand in a room—barren walls and floor of concrete—the
windows—boarded over—

I circle her—heels sharply clicking—

My fingertips—satin gloved—along shoulder blades—
gooseflesh—Long black hair—I pull aside—the skin and
soft light hairs—I put my lips to her skin—downy—I

whisper into her ear—*Nobody will ever find you*—How she struggles now—strains—I would like to—crack her across the face—But I would need to remove my glove—to feel—skin sting against skin—How slowly I draw off my glove—How sharp the crack of—skin against skin—Her eyes—confused—wounded—with tears—welling—

In a room—darkness—No—I see nothing—*What did you say to her*—Robert asks—My reply—whispered—*How quickly you learned*—Robert tells me—*It was always there*—I say—*waiting for you to*—pry it free—

Our little maid in the days to follow—Her pathetic light—dimming—She—sulks about—How suddenly now I reach for my teacup—to watch her flinch—

I fear we may have broken this one—Robert says—*How dreary she is become*—It is true—I feel some regret—*One learns a lesson in such ways*—I admit—*Yet*—I say—*I'd like to keep her*—

Yet I'd like to keep her—Can we not—paralyze her limbs—yet leave her mind quite—aware—Her flesh—suspended—requiring no more nourishment—activity—No more sulking for our girl housed in—a casket of glass—Yet her eyes lie—open—observing the—sun's passage—Shadow and light—the universe in motion—Moonlight now—a pale glow—branches—the wind howls—She hears the great organism of the house—groaning—electric current—heated water—heated—air—Her own organism—stilled—breathless—beatless—Every particle and atom—Even the microbes within will move—no more—

In this way I could—climb atop her—There perched—My eyes—moonlit—must gleam—a horrid silver—while I—poke and prod—Investigate—I pry open her mouth and her mouth must remain open—for my hand—wrist—Little maid—I will open you and climb within—I will know you entirely—Little maid—You will hide nothing

from me—Teeth and tongue—tonsils—spongy lungs—
Your heart—quieted—Through your eyes I will watch—the
light across the ceiling—crawl—languid motion—ether-
ized—I will know your every—desperate—terrified
thought—unheard cry—

On the screens—A man—gaunt—balding—bespeckled—
seated at a long table—in the German tongue he answers
his interrogators—*I hate no man*—he says—*no race—I could
have easily fled—til the end of time—I wanted this—To take
upon myself—the guilt of every German child—To answer
for my crimes—although I committed no crime—Atone for my
sins—although I have not sinned—My only sin—the virtue
of obedience—*

Did not your god—this man does not say—*demand of his
servant the unquestioning slaughter of a child—*

*Did not your god send my phantom soul through the vast-
ness—Exhale the vapor that sits before you—give it
shape—purpose—Did not your god impose upon me particular virtues—obedience—punctuality—efficiency—an even
temperament—Swelled me with ambition—Placed me in a
room with—particular men—set me to a—particular task—
Place me in any other world—and I am an accountant—But
your god—from its place adrift—set me in motion—from my
first cells' coalescence—Bid me—devour your—fathers and*

mothers—children—wives—Brought me to this room—aban-doned me—My neck will snap and my body swing because your god—dreamed it so—

*Here is a man who saw the world opened to him—*I do not tell Robert—*A man who—bathed blissfully in—soap of his victims—gifted his mistresses—rugs fashioned from—moun-tains of hair—Saw nothing in extermination but—a task to complete—*I do not say this—*Robert—this man woke no nights screaming—*

*I—Tiresias—He who was living is now dead—*Robert said—*Fear—a handful of—The barbarous king—nymphs—departed—I fed him carrots at dawn—stroked his flank—*Robert said—*Dead mountain mouth—Broken images—heaped—Your shadow at morning—your shadow—rising—I should like to swim in the sea—We could be happy there—*Robert said—*Dead trees—White bodies—the low damp ground—I am not afraid of death—*Robert said—*I am however afraid of the—human imbecile—Let them—asphyxiate and roast in their—fallout shelters—*Robert said—*Those hooded hordes—*Robert said—*swarming—The chemist said it would be all right—lidless eyes—*Robert said—*Marie—*Robert said—*Marie—hold on—The rattle of the bones—from ear to ear—Castro—Khruschev—missiles—*Robert said—*Kennedy—his head torn back—his mind—thrown—Co co rico co co rico—His lovely wife—how dignified she sat—My husband did so look forward to honoring you—Unreal City—Lamentation—maternal—a record—a gramophone—a mandolin—We were all hoodwinked—*Robert said—*seduced—We did not understand what an—insidious thing—The Red Menace—The communist—virus—A current under sea—picked his bones in—whispers—We who were living are now dying—They are listening to us—even now—*Robert said—*bugs in the walls—the phone—beneath the bed—One must be so careful these days—Dry bones can harm no one—*Robert said—*I was neither—Living nor dead—I knew nothing—Looking into the heart of light—*Robert said—*silence—I have not ridden a horse in twenty years—*Robert said—

I have not ridden a horse in twenty years—Robert said—*There is no day I do not think of it*—

Lovely—*chestnut*—*I fed her carrots at dawn*—*The desert at dawn*—*a blue light over the cracked earth*—*Others would shiver*—*chatter*—*for the morning cold*—*I did not*—

The long hours—*emptied of all save*—*silence itself*—*the horse's breathing*—*my own*—*the horse's footfalls*—*the rain*—*In such hours*—*ephemeral*—*serene*—*the body and mind*—*unify*—

Mountains—*red*—*Snows*—*Trails through*—*wilderness*—*fallen logs rotten*—*Deer nibbling*—*shrubbery*—*A fox*—*white and red pauses in its trot*—*A migration of tarantulas*—*tremendous sea*—*we watched from above*—*Whatever joys I have known are gone now save*—*within those recollections*—

In my death—*should I find such a place where*—*death is not*—

Let no one say Robert was not festive—Robert's tuxedo—Robert's cigarette—his martini—On the turntable—Tchaikovsky—*I abhor Tchaikovsky*—Robert says—

There are rooms lighted only by candles—dozens of tall candles—dripping—red, green, white—Robert admires the flames—*It is easy to see why so many women once died—wrapped in fire*—he jokes—The girl nearest the candles—steps back—

Several girls adorn the tree with tinsel, lights, garlands—red and silver—They are giggling—They are singing—Chestnuts Roasting—No—O Holy Night—White Christmas—They are—Robert—bids one girl come to him—she is dark haired—pale skin—*You have not been drinking your martini—little darling*—Robert says—tilts her glass so she must—swallow—*To the confusion of our enemies*—Robert says—

Before the feast—The long table—shrouded white—Robert at one head—I at the other—the girls—how eager their eyes—lips—There is mince pie—oyster bisque—baked ham—sweet potatoes—cranberry sauce—chestnuts—One girl has roasted a goose—Before the feast—Robert must speak—*Today we pay homage to the dead god—its miraculous birth*—Robert says—*Travelers came to witness the child* *in its poverty—swaddled in rags—nested in straw—Travelers bestow—treasures—fragrant—glowing—They called it King—Emperor of All Flesh—*Robert says—Robert sips his martini—Robert gestures for the girls to—listen intently—*Consider now the child's confusion—*Robert says—*A holy object, eternal, omnipotent—removed from its place in the vastness—smothered in mortal flesh—The child knows not its own name—the child knows all names—The dead god's—holy confusion—universe mysterious—*Robert pauses—drinks—*Its infant eyes processes as the world—dim shapes—shadows—colors—The child comprehends—every microbe—conceives already—its own oblivion—The oblivion of all light—Light conceived within its god-mind—*Robert says—*The child—for the first time—exists not—beyond the atom—as—originator and conceiver—No—the child—*Robert says—*is finally now—composed of—throttled within—atoms—Every speck unseen containing within—the tremendous annihilating spark—the dead god itself—*

Our summer along the ocean—Robert narrates stories of—worlds unseen—horrors—*Great whales*—Robert says—*hundreds of years aged*—*wash ashore*—*lie bloating and rotting*—*eyes larger than the largest man who stands to pick at the meat*—*Mysterious death*—*its flesh stripped away by*—*vast tentacles*—*The Kraken*—Robert says—*is quite real*—

Many hours—I simply watch—the lines of water—rippling—Many hours—I fall—into the horizon—

We eat—seafood salad—salt—lime—whenever we hunger—when Robert does not forget to eat—Fish—lobster—crabs—Martinis—Marlboros—Robert trudging barefooted along the shore—Robert drawing the lines from the waters—Robert—shirtless—burned tan—Robert—wasting away—skin, muscle, bone—organs thrumming—Robert—tireless—insatiable—in motion—constant—

Robert on the anniversary of his bomb—gestures to the horizon—the long blue line—You can almost see it—he says—Some guests strain their eyes—He has hired a band—trumpets—a guitar—They play—something festive—then—ominous—Robert then speaks—*The mysteries of the universe were then to us only*—*faintly known*—*yet I was determined*—

Robert—now—nothing but ash—urn—Porcelain vessel—
Robert now—less than ash—The face of the waters—gray
with Robert—*Meaningless gesture*—I think—*empty discol-
oration*—*May he finally find peace*—a woman says—*What a
horrible thing to say*—I think—

There are times Robert does not know himself—There are
times Robert only knows what he was—

This hotel—he says—*a wonder to behold*—Electric
lights—working telephones—in every room—Elevators—
remarkable ascent—creaking and groaning—the boy draws
open the fence—*Your floor*—*Sir*—Marble wainscotting—
Gold leaf—The Red Lacquer Room—There are—silver
dollars in the—barbershop floor—

On the kitchen floor—a bottle of milk—emptying—On the
kitchen floor—Robert—lips milky—moaning—His brow—
nose—cheeks—chin—streaked—bloody—Robert in his
bathrobe—fallen open—Robert shriveled—disappearing—
Floor tiles—tile cracks—pooled—white and red—Robert
has pissed himself—defecated—In his clarity he tells me—
Hold the pillow to my face—*fast*—*press until*—*you lie beside me
gasping*—*My limbs will fight you darling*—*I will not*—In his
confusion he says—*I could stand if I wanted to*—*although he
makes no movement to stand*—*My dear doctor*—he says—*stab
me now!*—*I will feel nothing*—

Two girls see Robert cleaned—his robe thrown out—his cut disinfected—bandaged—He lies in bed—bandage reddening—too weak to snore—A dog so afflicted—we would shoot—Robert—however—must continue—

Another girl—mopping the kitchen floor—I crack her across the face—She knows better than to meet my eyes—*Look at me*—I say—I crack her again—again—*Look at me—you fool*—She is—fallen to her knees—simpering—*Idiot cow*—I say—

Yet—Robert is—nothing now—I—alone—in his great house—The maid—notwithstanding—She is always—somewhere—scratching about—

Here—what was long ago called the ballroom—Fine young ladies—public debuts—white silk—satin—tulle—necklines—high—They dance the German—Young men—detrimental—indefatigable—indispensable—to them attend—Fine young ladies—youth—beauty—splendor—Dancing—flirting—Forever now—locked within—their hour of—potentiality—realized—They are all dead now—or lie discarded in—attic spaces—festering—

Here—Robert's library—He would lead me along the shelves—heap my arms with—volumes I would never read—*Grown quiet at the name of love*—Robert said—*the last embers of daylight—die—*

His office—Nobody was allowed enter—Girls left—trays of coffee, eggs, toast—in the hallway—Only once was I summoned—He stood before a window—his nose nearly pressed to the glass—*Come—hurry—But quietly*—he whispered—*Look*—he motioned through the window—rose bushes and flower beds and—hedge creatures—gravel paths—fountains—cherubs—bow and arrow—cock miniscule—Robert watched me—frantic eyes—I could say nothing other than—*What a lovely day—No*—he whispered—*Hoover's boys*—*Do you not see them*—I peered and peered—*Robert dear*—I said—*I see only the gardener*—Robert's eyes—burned—He gripped my forearm—*We have no gardener*—he hissed—

Here—in this room—General Washington plotted the slaughter of his own men—farmboys—blacksmiths—He wore his medals to bed—they all did—And here slept the general's servants—dreaming the general's murder—

This room—where Robert would—with straight razor—make smooth—my legs—long slow strokes—Now—my pussy—How tender he is in these moments—His concentration—His—breaths—The air against—my new skin—*I need you as if—newly born*—he says—

Here I was—tied to a chair—while upon a bed—another woman—She struggled against her bounds—writhed—And here I pressed my nose to the wall while I was—lashed raw—until I could no more sit—

This room—a room of mirrors—the ceiling—walls—Here I am—every angle—Breasts—neck—chin—Buttocks—belly—thighs—What would Robert say—*How grotesque you are—Every pockmark and wrinkle—every—sagging fold of meat*—Perhaps he wouldn't even look at me—He would—smell it—the aging—Yet—I think—he needed me—

Here I was—hooded—my mouth—stuffed with rags—A device—over my ears—affixed—Now I hear not my own moans—breathing—sighs—Now I hear—Sounds disembodied—footfalls—machinery—roaring—Robert's voice—yet—not—*If you were a lovely boy*—he says—*I would lock you in a room—furnished with only a mattress of straw—At night—candlelight—your body—rise and fall—Beautiful lad— Hips—smooth bones—rosey—Your face so still it might—never again move—*

This is the room where Robert kept his photographs—Street girls he fed—steaks and asparagus—Coeds—awed by the—great man—The daughters of diplomats—scientists—senators—

This is the room where we hanged them by their arms—ropes—creaking—How quickly—one's arms—numb—

This is where I drew the rope—taut—Long, lithe—necks—*Leave a mark*—Robert said—

This is the room where I lashed them until I could lift my arms no more—It cut the air—Spray of blood—sweat—my own sweat—Smiling—gasping—blood in my mouth—Robert in his chair—smoking—Robert's trousers to his ankles—Robert's wide grin—

This is the tub I filled with water—shoved their stupid—sputtering—faces—into—They cannot thrash for wrists—ankles—bound—Robert leans in the doorway—humming Bach—blue haze of smoke—

This is the chair where I sat while Robert directed them to—pleasure me—How wide my legs spread—the treasure—opened—Their tongues—pink—hesitant—dumbly lapping—*Do not be afraid dear*—I told them—My hand upon the back of their head—nest of hair—pushing them in—deeper—

These are the rooms where they slept—dreamt perhaps of home—escape—

Each to their own little room—beds—nightstands—wardrobes—Secluded—Separated by—walls—doors—Robert did not want them to—congregate—plot—

No windows—Robert does not want them to—see the world—unless we—show them the world—No light—unless we decree—there is light—

Days of darkness—They weep—beat on walls— soundproof—Hands search surfaces—for cracks—openings—weaknesses—We give them paper—pencils—They write messages—slide them under the door—Their first missives— illegible—filthy—cluttered—They became adept at—composition sightless—Letters—plead- ing—*The stench*—they say—*overwhelms*—*The terror*—Then—we give them light—they cry out—Shocked—blinded—On the screens—we watch them—cowering in the corners—

They have no sound save their own—voices—fists beating bloody against floors—walls—Their own— breathing—capillaries—organs—Then we give them sound—noise immense—Robert reading slowly— patiently—*rhythmically*—in Greek—Latin—recorded to tape—spooled—replayed—for hours—days—Then we give them—Wagner—Carl Orff—*Louder*—Robert says—turning the knob until it—turns no more—

When they are—simpering—obliterated—We fill them with rags—hood them—bind their wrists—

Are you speaking—or am I—Robert asks a girl—her hood— removed—*Are you this woman in blood—or am I*—He strokes her hair from her eyes—*You see this world of light I have built—Here we—wear many masks—histories*—He calls her by the name we have given her—Refers to the family we have for her—invented—This world—nameless— immortal—burns—towering—it will swallow itself—the universe—

There are floors I could not before—access—Darkened hallways—I had never before seen—How many years I have lived here—still the hallways—strange—alien—How many rooms even I have not visited—One could make a lifetime of—opening doors—entering—exiting—Finding iterations of one's self—Newly existent yet—in existence perpetually—vaporous yet—substantial—

In this room I stand—myself—yet not—She smiles— without surprise—as if she has expected me the while—Ornamented—diamonds—pearls—You see—How many years since I last wore—the silver gown she wears now—Line of neck—collarbone—*You have been here—all this while*—I insist—When she replies—it is nothing I would not say—

Now—a new room—Now—another version of—Here I pace—murmuring—Always—new rooms—new iterations—Here I squat in Robert's great chair—the screen flickers—a burning monk—my eyes—smoke and flame—Here I sleep—How peaceful I have been—once submerged—In the doorways of—all rooms—I call to her— *Clara*—In some—she turns to me—smiling—In some—she insists upon—a different name—*Clarice—Candace—Cara*— In some—she insists—*You are nothing like I am*—In some rooms—she whispers—*Robert is coming—you must go*—The door—quickly shut—Here I linger—listening—Is that Robert's voice—again—after all these years—or—a recording only—

Here is the one I want—Here I lie—casketed—rosewood—How peaceful—hands over my breast—folded—elegant lilies—Over her I lean—mirrored—Yet not—I would unthread her eyes—so she may see—Her mouth—so she may speak—So there— sounds from within the chamber—struggling—*What have you seen*—I ask—*What dreams have you—inside the chasm—How long has it been—five days—a dozen years*—Does she murmur her reply—Perhaps she describes—wandering—mysterious corridors—no—No sound from oblivion is permitted—return—

Here there are rooms for all the girls we have known—Our little maids—

Here—heaped—limbs tangled—broken—rotten—Faces—what were faces—caverns—skeletal—

Sweet child—which were you—Lipless—trapped in this—realm—breathless—voice no more—Where once the navel—a mossy—festering—What were breasts—I did surely fondle—stroke—suckle—bite—You bled—I drank— What were breasts—moldering—green and black—What was flesh—a mucus pulp—pulled aside—breastbone and ribs—

Here—As they were when they first came to us—How naive they were—untouched—pure—I suddenly desire them gone—*Run*—I might command—No—How futile—for I would only—fall upon them again—*Climb out the windows if you must*—I tell them—only to drag them back by— kicking feet—loose shoes fall—to the floor—No action on their part or mine can save them—The kindly gesture is wasted thought—They can flee this great house—Run along country roads—crying for help—They can return to their apartment houses—tenement rooms—They believe themselves—saved—No—There is nothing they can do—Oblivion will find them—We are already there—

Perhaps—in some room further—I will find Robert's device—Encased in steel—mechanism bulbous—yellow and black—One senses the—maelstrom in wait—*It vexed us*— Robert said—*the problem—a device small enough to deliver through the air—powerful enough to—destroy a city*—In this room—Robert's device—hovers—suspended by no—rope or wire—hums—throbs—The universe within—split—All possible worlds—burning—I want to stand before it—pleading—*When will you exhale—Bring us—cataclysm—Swallow us all—in light—*

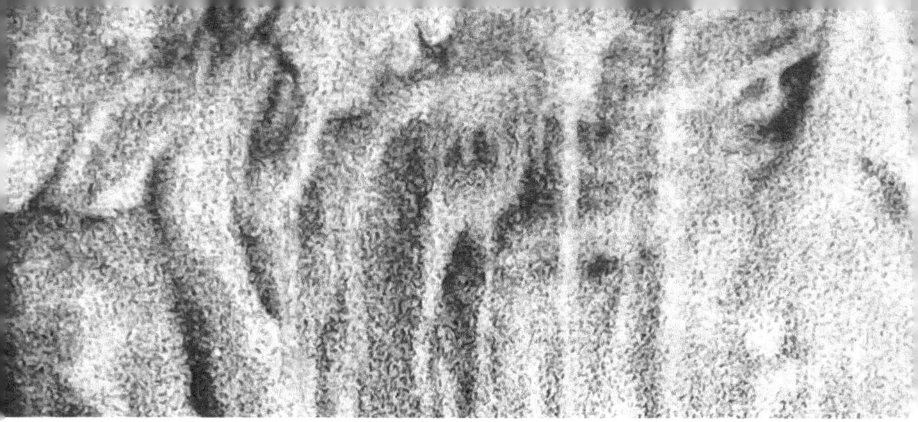

Postscript

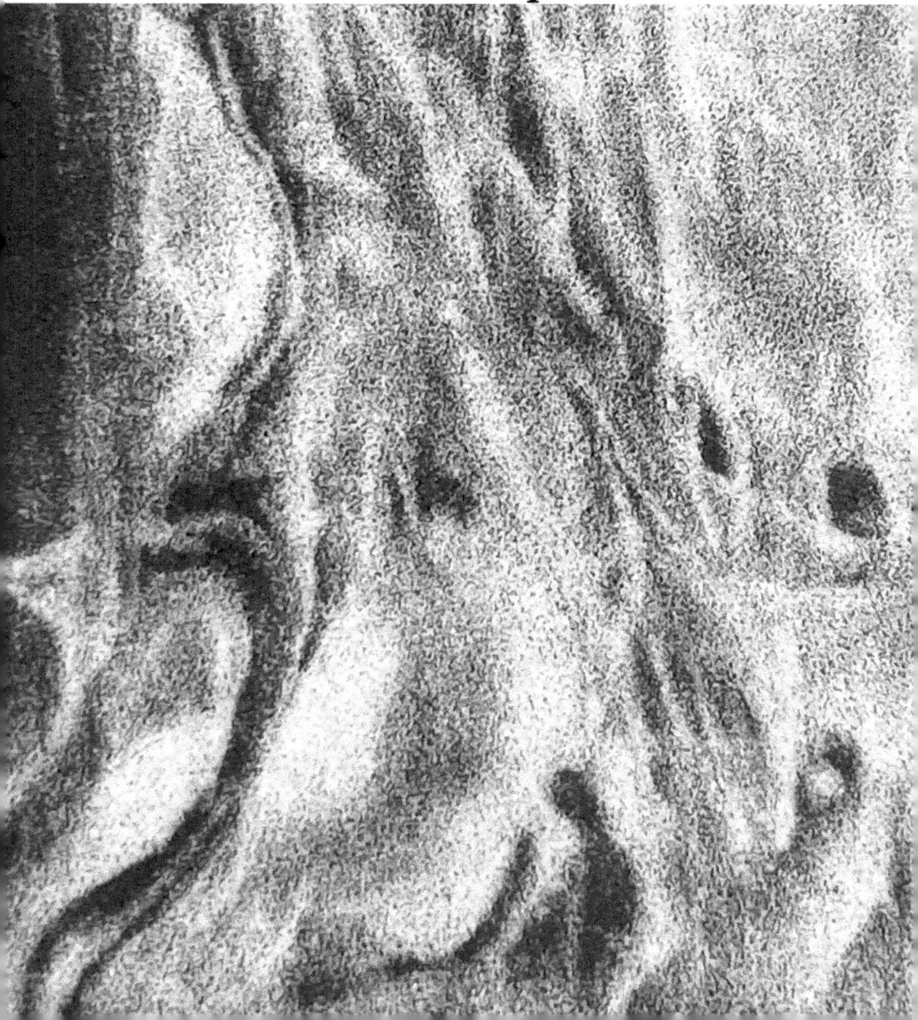

There are many rooms—they peel away—Cities atop of cities—Cities of oil—napalm—fire—

Maybe now—there will be liberty—he said—

I had no choice—he said—my hand was forced—

Cities of—shock tubes—Tovex Blastrite Gel—ammonium nitrate fertilizer—nitromethane—diesel fuel—Cities of— screaming—burning—Flesh—mutilated—by glass—explosive force—debris—Cities—men—women—children—torn to pieces—scorched—limbs—scattered—

—a mass casualty event—

—sic semper tyrannis—he said—the tree of liberty—the blood of tyrants—Ruby Ridge—he said—Waco, Texas—he said—

Nineteen dead children—collateral damage—he said— The nature of the beast—If there is a hell—he said—I'll improvise—adapt—overcome—

—events—variations—transmutations—Here what was life—removed of life—Here—life no more—There are many

rooms—

They peel away—

BASEMENT TAPES 010374-010383

The tape is shut off—The tape is started—

Slender boy—gawky—smiling—What is he in his mind—
We are no longer human—he says—We're—self aware—He
wears—black BDU's—no shirt—He is—holding a shotgun—
It's a weird feeling—he says—knowing you're going to be dead
in two weeks—He says—should we do it before—or after—the
prom—

Silent now—he wipes away a tear—It's humans that I hate—he
says—

I'm sorry I have so much rage—I really am sorry about all of
this—But war's war—

Brandon Larson—they say— The suburbs—they say—Blacks—
feminists—born again Christians—jocks—people who wear

Tommy Hilfiger clothes—Dustin—everything you say is point-less—Nick—you laugh too much—Rachel—Jen—Christianic bitches—I'm gonna shoot you in the head—

When you find his jaw—one says—it won't be on his face—

I just know I want to kill the fuckers who fucked with me—one says—Tick, tick, tick, tick, tick—the other says—

The tape is shut off—The tape is started—The tape is—

You can find anything on the internet—they say—how to make—bombs, poison, napalm—how to buy guns if you're underage—

3 hours 1 minute 55 seconds of footage—

They say—only two weeks left—They say—propane bombs—containers—pouches to load shells in—They say—devices—propane tanks—They say—bomb holders—Radio Shack—a clock—speaker— a solar—ignitor—
We are—but we aren't—psycho—

Item #200 Sony 8mm video camera serial #74415

—my bandolier of stuff—napalm—

Doom—they say—KMFDM—

I am full of hate—one wrote—I love it—I want to die really bad right now—the other wrote—

Item #265 8mm Tape

—solar igniters, engines, batteries, clocks, pipes—completed pipe bombs—

Fucking bitches—

Megan—Karen—Tanya—Cindy—Katie—Sara—Mandy—

The tape is shut off—The tape is turned on—
One says—Say it now—The other says—Hey mom—gotta go—I just want to apologize to you guys—I'll be happier wherever the fuck I go—So I'm gone—The other says—Everyone I

love—I'm really sorry about all this—mom—dad—I'm sorry—I can't help it—

One says—Morris—Nate—If you guys live—I want you to have what you want—the other says—You can have my stuff too—

That's it—one says—sorry—goodbye—the other says—goodbye—

The tape is shut off—

They step into a world beyond the knowable—flashes of light— They become—security footage—eye witness accounts—distant sounds—They were laughing—it is said—when they entered the library—

An American Nightmare—a broadcaster says—We won't announce the killer's names—too often history remembers—lionizes—the murderers—while the victims are forgotten—

A city—shining—here the dead are housed—I have given your life meaning—the killer said—

—he passed before the camera—the tape here is warped—static burst—crackled—

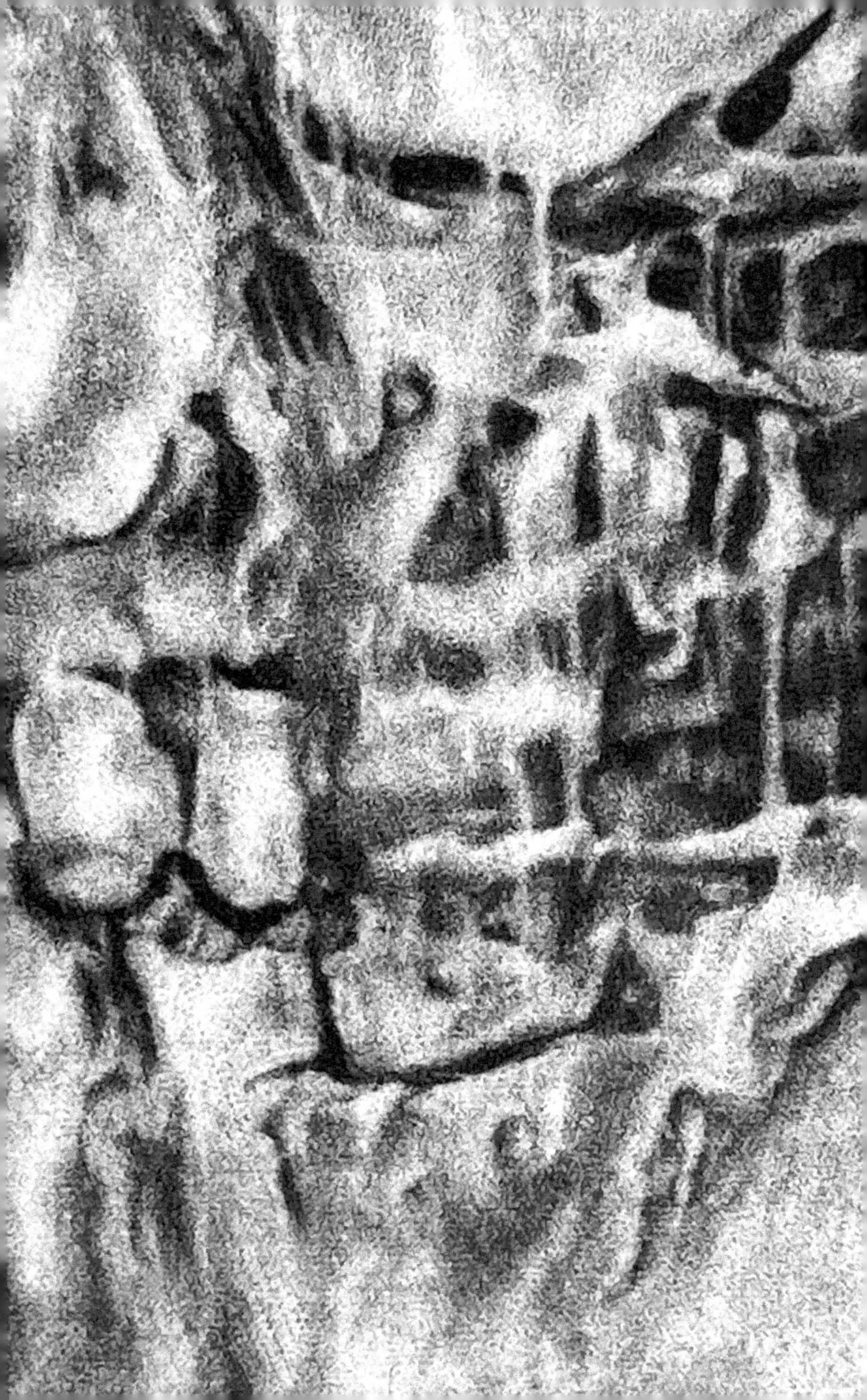